COCO PINCHARD'S MUST-HAVE TOY STORY

A SPARKLING, FEEL-GOOD CHRISTMAS NOVELLA

ROBERT BRYNDZA

RAVEN
STREET

Raven Street Publishing
www.ravenstreetpublishing.com
© Raven Street Limited 2021

eBook ISBN: 978-1-914547-04-1
Print ISBN: 978-1-8384878-4-3
ALSO AVAILABLE AS AN AUDIOBOOK

For Ján, with who I'm lucky enough to celebrate Christmas twice each year!

DECEMBER 1992

MONDAY 14TH DECEMBER

I was late to work this morning. I'm the teacher who lives the closest to school, so that made it even more embarrassing.

When I opened the door to my form room, the Headmaster, Mr Sutcliffe, was behind my desk taking registration. This was bad. He *never* sets foot in a classroom. I waited nervously at the back until he'd finished calling the register.

'And Mrs Pinchard,' he said, looking up at me with his cold blue eyes.

'Present,' I said, automatically. 'I mean, thank you Headmaster. I'm now here, obviously.'

I scurried to the front of the class, under the smirking gaze of thirty-two fourteen-year-olds. Mr Sutcliffe's first name is Peter, which has earned him the nickname 'The Ripper'.

'I'm terribly sorry I'm late, Headmaster,' I said, unwinding my scarf and setting down my bag. He was silent: he expected me to make my excuses in front of the kids. 'It's been a rather disorganised morning,' I added, lowering my voice.

'How, exactly?' he asked, sitting back in my chair.

The reason I was late was because Rosencrantz had been showing us extracts from his forthcoming primary school Nativity play at the breakfast table. He'd even made up a song and performed it standing on his chair, accompanied by me and Daniel tapping our cutlery enthusiastically against a bowl and an empty milk bottle:

> *I'm the bestest and wisest man,*
> *Ten times better than Peter Pan,*
> *I've got lots of Frankincense,*
> *I got it on offer for fifty pence,*
> *Is that Jesus in his pram?*
> *He looks like a lump of boiled ham!*

Most mornings I have to leave the house as Rosencrantz is eating his breakfast. It kills me to think what silliness and fun I've missed out on. I just couldn't miss his little Wise Man song, and I'm so glad I didn't. Daniel and I were crying with laughter.

I realised The Ripper was still staring at me, waiting for an answer, along with the kids in my class.

'My road was closed off by the police. No one was allowed out,' I lied. He cocked his head, waiting to hear more. I went on, 'I don't know *why* they closed it, perhaps it was a gas leak, or a drug raid... or a prostitution ring...' The kids began to snigger. 'Not that I live in that kind of area, of course, Headmaster. Or that I would be involved in a prostitution ring. I've barely enough time to finish all my marking!' I joked.

The kids laughed. The Ripper's mouth was now set in a grim line.

'SILENCE!' he yelled.

The kids were instantly still and quiet. A vein was throbbing in his temple.

'Mrs Pinchard,' he said, in a dangerously low tone, 'I was walking past your form room and your class was running wild. Someone was exposing their bare bottom, and pressing it against the glass partition. Unfortunately I was unable to identify the culprit.' I bit my lip, suppressing the urge to laugh. He went on, 'You should have phoned the school secretary and informed me you wouldn't be here to take registration. Don't ever do that again.'

I shivered as he rose and left with the register. When he'd gone, my class had a field day.

'Uuummmm, Miss. You're *so* in trouble!' said Kelly Roffey, swinging back on her chair.

'Did you see that vein throbbing, Miss? He was really pissed off,' said Damian Grange.

'I'm not surprised. Now, who was it who flashed their bum at the Headmaster?' I asked.

'It was Damian, Miss,' said Kelly Roffey.

'Prove it,' said Damian.

'Miss, Damian's arse has seven pimples... get him to drop his trousers and you'll see,' said Kelly Roffey.

'No one is dropping their trousers, now quiet,' I snapped.

I wasn't surprised that Damian was the culprit. I was surprised, however, that Kelly Roffey could count to seven.

I can't quite believe I've ended up as an English teacher. I thought it would be fun. I thought I'd spend all day discussing my favourite literature. But the truth is, working at St Dukes Comprehensive is mostly crowd control. I don't know how to inspire a load of petulant teenagers.

'Quiet,' I said, wiping the blackboard. 'Now, for

homework, I asked you to read the first two chapters of *A Christmas Carol*.'

They all groaned and pulled out their books.

'What were your first impressions of Mr Scrooge? What is he like as a character?' I asked.

Blank faces stared back at me.

'Come on, this is *A Christmas Carol*. We've all heard the phrase *to be a Scrooge...*'

'Miss? My copy's got pages missing,' said Kelly Roffey. 'It says nothing about Bob Cratchit being a frog.'

'That's *The Muppet Christmas Carol*,' I sighed.

'Oh. Is the book different?' asked Kelly, sincerely.

The class broke down into catcalls and laughter.

At lunchtime I collapsed into an armchair in the staffroom. A half bald Christmas tree was balanced on a plastic crate by the door, swaying woozily as teachers rushed past to get in the queue for the tea urn.

The curtains were clamped shut against the grey winter sky. Under the window opposite me sat three teachers eating their sandwiches: Miss Bruce (Maths, longest-serving staff member), Mr Gutteridge (Humanities, stinks of wee and coffee) and Miss Rolincova (Science, a new teacher like me, but unlike me she's from Slovakia and incredibly beautiful). She caught me staring at her, and I quickly looked away.

The dreary silence was broken by Miss Mesere, the French teacher. Elegant and always beautifully dressed, she sashayed past us all in a tight red skirt and jacket, her sleek dark hair swept back in a bun. She exists on a different plane to the rest of us. Her husband is minted, an investment banker

I think, and she teaches French to keep busy. She was carrying a posh cake box from Patisserie Valerie, and a plastic bag with a boxed Tracy Island toy poking out of the top. She put the plastic bag down and opened the fridge.

Mrs Carter (Geography, perpetually exhausted, has five boys) came up behind her.

'Good God, how did you get hold of one of those?' she asked.

'Zis is for ma 'usband. Crème caramel. 'Is favorit,' Miss Mesere smiled, making space for the cake box in the tiny fridge.

'Not the cake, the Tracy Island,' Mrs Carter said. 'May I?'

Miss Mesere nodded, and Mrs Carter pulled out the Tracy Island toy, merchandise from *Thunderbirds*, the TV show for kids.

'Where the hell did you get it? There's a huge shortage of these toys!' exclaimed Mrs Carter.

'A fabulous little toyshop near ze Kings Road,' said Miss Mesere. 'French, of course. Monsieur Fauchon, 'ow do you say? 'E *put one on ze side* for me.'

She plucked the Tracy Island from the envious Mrs Carter's grip, slid it back in the plastic bag, and sashayed out of the staffroom with a smile.

'What do you mean, there's a huge shortage?' I asked.

'You must have heard, Mrs Pinchard, surely,' said Mrs Carter coming over to our group of chairs. 'All the toyshops have sold out of Tracy Islands... You've got a little boy, haven't you?'

'Yes. Rosencrantz is four,' I said, remembering with horror that he'd already written his Christmas letter, and he'd asked for Tracy Island.

Mr Gutteridge pulled out a crumpled copy of *The Sun*,

and smoothing it out on the stained coffee table, started to read out loud from an article.

"This year's must-have Christmas toy is the Tracy Island playset, but toyshops up and down the country have run out. The factory in China, where the toys are made, can't keep up with demand. However, *Blue Peter* is coming to the rescue! Tune in at teatime when they'll be showing parents how to make their own version of Tracy Island using cardboard boxes and empty washing-up liquid bottles," he read, adding, 'Blimey, what kid would want a homemade one?'

'I think me and the hubby are going to have to make *five*. Our boys are all Thunderbirds crazy,' sighed Mrs Carter.

'Who is this Blue Peter?' asked Miss Rolincova.

'Blue Peter isn't a person,' snapped Miss Bruce, peeling a black banana. 'It's a children's television programme on BBC One...'

'Surely there must be some Tracy Islands in the shops?' I said desperately.

'Nope. There are only two moulds in the factory, apparently,' said Mr Gutteridge peering at *The Sun*. 'Sounds like the Chinks have been caught on the hop!'

'Mr Gutteridge, you can't say that!' clucked Mrs Carter indulgently.

Miss Rolincova stood up, brushed the crumbs off her black skirt and left, giving us all an awkward nod.

Mrs Carter waited till she'd gone, then turned back to our group saying, 'She's making no effort to integrate...'

'There are plenty of *English* people who can teach science,' sneered Miss Bruce, a banana string hanging off the corner of her mouth. 'Why did the Headmaster have to hire an Eastern European?'

'I had a cracking night with an Eastern European girl once,

she could suck a golf ball through a hose pipe!' said Mr Gutteridge, rolling up his copy of *The Sun*. Mrs Carter chuckled indulgently.

I ignored them all and was about to go and phone Daniel when The Ripper came into the staffroom. He was flanked by Miss Marks, the young school secretary, who was holding a stack of plastic buckets. They stopped beside the Christmas tree, and a hush descended.

'I don't wish to disturb your lunch, but I do want to remind you all that tomorrow is our Christingle assembly,' he said. 'We're honoured and privileged to have the Lord Mayor of London attending with his Lady Mayoress.'

There was silence from the unimpressed, mainly socialist staff.

'*And* the School Governors,' he continued. 'Staff must ensure each student in their class brings an orange to decorate, and explain the significance of the Christingle to them.'

'Most of my class don't even know what an orange is, let alone the significance of the bloody Christingle,' I murmured.

'Did you want to say something, Mrs Pinchard?' asked The Ripper, fixing his cold eyes on me.

'No, Headmaster,' I said, going bright red.

'I thought perhaps you were volunteering to help? We need someone to supervise the students with their oranges and candles.'

'Erm...' I began.

'Shall I put Mrs Pinchard down for oranges and candle lighting?' asked Miss Marks with a nasty smile.

'Yes, do, she's obviously very keen,' said The Ripper. There was an awkward pause. He went on, 'Staff will also need to co-ordinate a charity collection for any spare change.

I'm confident we can beat last year's total of ninety-seven pounds.'

Everyone stared at him. More work before the end of term.

'Thank you. I'll leave Miss Marks to assign the charity buckets,' said The Ripper.

When he'd gone, the staffroom burst back into a noisy chatter.

'Bad luck, Mrs Pinchard. Let's hope there isn't a repeat of last year's Christingle assembly,' said Mrs Carter.

'What happened last year?' I asked.

'Two pupils ended up in hospital with burns. Shelley Martin's perm went up like the *Hindenburg*.'

'And what about the other pupil?' I asked.

'Dean Lewis spent three weeks in hospital after he tried to light one of his farts. It was like that film, *Backdraft*,' said Mrs Carter.

On cue the bell rang, and everyone trooped back to their form rooms.

I arrived home just after five, exhausted. It was dark and cold, and light was glowing softly against the closed curtains of the living room. When I opened the front door I could hear the end of *Newsround*. I put my bag down in the hall and poked my head around the living room door. Rosencrantz was sitting atop his favourite beanbag, his tiny legs poking out with his *Thunderbirds* slippers on.

'Mummy, Mummy, Mummy!' he shouted, leaping up and grabbing at my legs. He'd left a tiny imprint in the beanbag, like the well in a cake mix where you break the egg. I lifted him up and he kissed my cheeks and gave me a hug.

'How was school?' I asked.

'Today I ate all my dinner, even though it was a bit cold... and Melanie Jones was told off for filling up the toilet with loo roll... and we had the rehearsals for the Nativity play. Joseph can't remember his lines.'

'But you know all yours?'

'Of course I know all my lines, Mummy,' he said seriously.

'And you've got your brilliant song. Did you sing it for everyone?'

'No, Mummy. I only made that up to make you and Daddy laugh. I have to stick to the script. Even if I only have to bring the Frankincense,' he said, rolling his little eyes as if his talents were being squandered as a mere Wise Man.

'You are going to be the best, wisest Wise Man,' I said.

'It's going to be a big production,' he added, like a seasoned pro. 'Mrs Masters is lending her four Dulux dogs for the manger scene. They've just had their hair cut so they look a bit like camels.'

'It sounds... interesting,' I said.

We looked up as *Blue Peter* started on the television.

'Mummy! They're making a Tracy Island on Blue Peter! Am I going to get Tracy Island for Christmas?'

Bugger, bugger, bollocks, I thought.

'You posted your letter to Father Christmas?' I asked.

He nodded furiously. 'I licked the stamp and everything!'

'Then of course you're going to get Tracy Island for Christmas.' *You're a rotten lying mother,* said a voice in my head.

Rosencrantz did a little jiggle of happiness then climbed back into his dent in the beanbag. On the TV in the corner of the living room, Anthea Turner was dressed in her fluffy *Blue Peter* jumper and listing all the bits you needed to make a

Tracy Island at home. I stood by the door and watched Rosencrantz's happy little face for a moment, then went through to the kitchen.

Daniel was sitting at the kitchen table. He looked up and gave me a grin. His mother was standing by the sink in her flowery housecoat.

'Hello Ethel, I didn't know you were coming over, again?' I said, trying to keep my voice light.

'Didn't know I 'ad to make an appointment?' she said. She picked up the teapot, swilled it round and tipped cold tealeaves down the sink.

'Course you don't, Ethel. You just seem to be in town a lot lately,' I said, kissing Daniel on top of his head.

'Mum came up to town to get her ears syringed,' he explained.

'Was it a success? Has it improved your eavesdropping skills?' I asked.

'Thought I'd pop in see my favourite boys... An' you, love, of course,' said Ethel.

We gave each other an insincere smile.

'How was your day?' I asked Daniel, putting my arm round him.

'I got the final version of the music score sent off to the pantomime company for *Dick Whittington*. I hope they like it,' he said.

'They'll love it,' I told him.

'Oh Coco, you got another rejection letter fer one of yer stories,' said Ethel, banging down the teapot on the worktop.

'Sorry Cokes, I opened it by mistake,' said Daniel. He searched through a pile of bills on the kitchen table and handed me a letter from *The People's Friend* magazine. I quickly scanned it, noting it said the short story I'd submitted wasn't suitable for publication. I'd *almost* got used to the rejection letters these days. I sighed and tucked it back amongst the pile of bills.

'What is it they say? Don't give up yer day job?' asked Ethel.

'Now Mum, Coco's a wonderful writer, she just hasn't had her break yet,' said Daniel.

I pulled the kitchen door shut and fished *The Sun* out of my bag.

'Look, forget about that. We need to talk. Have you seen the paper?' I said, smoothing it out on the kitchen table.

'I know. Poor Princess Diane, splitting up with that Charles,' said Ethel, spooning fresh tealeaves into the pot. 'She won't leave the Royal Family and come out alive.'

Why is Ethel the only person in the world who calls her Princess Diane?

'Who'd want to hurt Princess *Diana*?' I asked.

'She gave the Queen an Anus Horribilis,' explained Ethel.

'It's *Annus Horribilis*,' I corrected.

'Well, whatever it is, it sounds painful,' said Ethel. 'That Diane should watch 'er back, tha's all I'm saying.'

The kettle clicked off and she poured hot water into the pot. I resisted the urge to press the Diana/Diane debate.

'Anyway, I'm not talking about Diana. Look!' I said.

I opened the newspaper and flicked through to the page about Tracy Island. Ethel came over to the table and she and Daniel both peered at the article in silence. Ethel's lips moved as she read.

'Blimey,' said Daniel, sitting back and reaching for a cigarette.

'Coco, iss only a week or so till Christmas! What 'ave you bin doing for the past two months?' exclaimed Ethel.

'I've been at work! You've spent the past two months on the bus up here and back to Catford. You could have jumped off at Hamleys, Ethel,' I retorted.

'I've been up and down to the 'ospital with all sorts, Coco. I've got a bad back, bad hips...'

'And there's all that earwax,' I said.

'Okay you two,' said Daniel. 'Let's go outside and have a cigarette.'

'The door's shut, Danny, the smoke won't reach little Rosencrantz,' said Ethel.

'No. We smoke outside, Ethel,' I said.

We grabbed our coats and reconvened on the terrace. The moon was now up and the lawn had frozen and was glistening in the moonlight.

'Maybe we can persuade Rosencrantz to like another toy. What about Action Man?' suggested Daniel.

'We could make a Tracy Island? They were just on *Blue Peter*, using toilet rolls and margarine tubs,' I began.

'You can't give 'im something made up of all the old shit you'd throw away!' said Ethel. She had a point.

There was a knock on the door and Rosencrantz pressed his nose against the glass.

'Everybody, I just thought up a funny Thunderbirds joke!' he shrilled.

We stubbed out our cigarettes and came back inside, relishing the warmth from the kitchen.

'Go on, tell us yer joke, love,' said Ethel.

Rosencrantz took a deep breath.

'Why is Parker called Parker?'

'I don't know, why is Parker called Parker?' I asked.

'Cos he's a good parker!' Rosencrantz cried, grinning with his little row of milk teeth. Ethel and I laughed.

'Oooh! Tha's funny!' she said, scooping him up for a cuddle.

Only Daniel remained confused.

'Who's Parker?' he asked.

'Oh Daddy, you're a ding-dong dilly noodle,' said Rosencrantz. 'Don't you know *anything*? Parker is Lady Penelope's chauffeur in *Thunderbirds*!'

Rosencrantz jumped down from Ethel's arms and started to swan round the kitchen, doing a rather brilliant Lady Penelope voice and jigging gently as if he were suspended from strings.

'Parker, we appear to have intruders. I think they are going to take my jewels,' he said. *'Yes, M'lady, but h'I fink we might be unable to stop 'em,'* he said, switching to an equally good impression of Parker. 'EVERYONE! I can't wait for Christmas Day! Thunderbirds are go, go, GO!' he shouted and ran round the kitchen and back through to the living room.

Ethel looked at me and raised an eyebrow.

'Right I've gotta be orf,' she said picking up her bag. She saw my despondent face. 'Don't worry Coco, love, we'll sort something out.'

'Yeah Cokes, there's still a few shopping days to go till Christmas,' added Daniel.

'Danny, be a good lad and walk yer old Mum round to the bus stop,' said Ethel.

When they'd gone, I cleared away all the bills. Then, pulling out a big pile of marking, I sat down at the kitchen table. When Daniel returned he brought fish and chips, and we ate them on our knees in front of the telly. Every time a silly Christmas advert came on Rosencrantz laughed with his little open mouth half full of chips, and me and Daniel looked at each other nervously.

'We should sort out the tree and the decorations too,' said Daniel quietly.

Later on, I'd just put Rosencrantz to bed when the phone rang. It was Ethel.

'Coco!' she whispered down the line. 'I've 'ad a tip-off... About this Tracy Island...'

I wasn't sure why she was whispering. She lives alone, and her next-door neighbour, Mrs Roberts, is deaf.

'Ask Danny if 'e remembers old Bert 'oo was in the pidgin fanciers with 'is dad?' she went on.

Daniel was coming out of the downstairs toilet with a magazine. I relayed the message and he leant into the receiver.

'Yeah Mum, I remember Bert,' he said.

'Well, Bert works for Conway's Lorries,' continued Ethel. "E's driving a load of them Tracy Islands up from Dover tomorrow morning fer the toyshops. And 'e's gonna stop in a lay-by an' a few are gonna fall off the back of 'is lorry... You know, cash. No questions.'

'That sounds illegal, Ethel,' I sniffed.

'Oh gawd, Coco. Do you want this Tracy Island for Rosencrantz or not?'

'Of course I do,' I said.

'Then this is 'ow we get it.'

'That's great, Mum!' said Daniel. 'Coco, you can drive, I'll read the map.'

'An' I'll be the go-between, me an' Bert go way back,' said Ethel.

'Hang on. I can't go to Dover tomorrow,' I protested. 'I've got to be at work! There's a special Christingle assembly... We're on pain of death if we don't show up.'

'You know I can't drive, Coco,' said Daniel.

'You should put yer son first, Coco. Before some bloody school assembly,' added Ethel.

I suddenly had a vision of Rosencrantz crying on Christmas Day under a present-less Christmas tree.

'Okay, I'll sort something out,' I sighed. 'What time should we leave tomorrow?'

'Bert said 'e'll be in the lay-by at 'alf ten, and iss first come first served, so we better make it early,' said Ethel.

TUESDAY 15TH DECEMBER

I still had some marking to do after we'd eaten our fish and chips. I took it up to bed to do and it was gone midnight when I finished, but I couldn't sleep. I was worried about phoning in sick for work, the repercussions of missing The Ripper's Christingle assembly, and Rosencrantz being without a present on Christmas Day. When I finally did sleep, I had a dream he was under the Christmas tree, tearing Christmas paper off a large present with a bow, which turned out to be an empty cornflakes box. He turned it upside down and a lone cornflake fell out onto the carpet. He looked up at me with tears in his eyes and said, 'Mummy, don't you love me?'

I woke suddenly. My heart was pounding and I saw by the glowing digital clock that it was three in the morning. I got up to go to the bathroom, slipped on the pile of exercise books I'd left by the bed, and went crashing forward, hitting my left eye on the brass doorknob. My howl of pain woke Daniel, and he leapt out of bed to find me squatting on the floor, clutching my eye.

'What is it, love? What did you do?' he asked, flicking on the light.

'I slipped over on those bloody stupid school books!'

He peered at my face and tilted my throbbing eye up to the light.

'The skin isn't broken, but you might have a shiner come morning,' he said. 'Let me get you some ice to put on your eye, and then you should come back to bed.'

He padded off downstairs and returned with some ice wrapped in a tea towel and two tumblers of whiskey. We climbed into bed and he put his arm round me.

'Christmas wasn't like this in the old days, was it?' I asked, leaning my head on his chest. I pressed the ice pack to my throbbing eye and grimaced.

'What do you mean?' said Daniel.

'There never used to be this one Christmas toy that everyone HAD to have. I remember getting a doll's pram, and another year I got a pretend iron and ironing board.'

'One year I got an Action Man, and everyone went bonkers over the fact his eyes could move from side to side,' said Daniel.

'Tracy Island apparently plays electronic sounds too. We'll have to remember batteries... Do you think we'll get one?'

'Course we will, Cokes. Mum's known this Bert bloke for years – he'll come through tomorrow, don't you worry,' said Daniel. 'And I can organise Christmas,' he added.

'You will? You'll do everything this year?'

'I promise. You don't need to lift a finger. I'll get the beds ready for when Meryl and Tony come to stay, and sort the tree, the decorations, the turkey. And I'll buy frozen. It won't be a live one,' he said. Despite everything, I laughed.

'That was the strangest Christmas, when Ethel brought a live turkey. I wish I'd taken a picture of my father's face,' I said.

'Mum couldn't face killing it...'

'She could quite happily kill me though,' I said, adding, 'She thinks I'm a bad mother, for going back to work.'

'Well, *I* know that you're doing it for us,' said Daniel. He pulled me close and gave me a kiss. 'You know, Cokes, Mum does love you too, deep down,' he added.

'It must be very deep down,' I sighed, taking a big gulp of whiskey. 'Daniel, could you have a word with her, nicely, and maybe suggest she doesn't have to be here every evening when I get home? Of course you should see your mother, but she's been here most days for the past four months and...'

There was the soft sound of snoring: Daniel had fallen asleep.

'You have perfect timing,' I said. I drank the last of my whiskey and tried to get comfortable, balancing the ice pack on my throbbing eye.

I woke at six the next morning with the alarm screaming and me soaking wet. The ice in the tea towel had melted. The only upside of all this was that I sounded suitably groggy when I phoned Miss Marks to say I wouldn't be at school.

'Mrs Pinchard, you do know it's the Christingle assembly?' said Miss Marks incredulously. I said I did. She asked me again what was wrong, and I repeated that I had been concussed.

'How *exactly*, Mrs Pinchard?' she asked sharply.

'It's none of your business how,' I snapped, losing my temper. 'I have a concussion, and I have been advised not to come in to work.'

Miss Marks never quite believes when a teacher is ill, so they tend to over-explain their symptoms. On several occasions a note has come through to the staffroom saying that someone will be off 'because they've been on the toilet all night'. I can't imagine this happens in a bank.

'The Headmaster won't be pleased,' she said. I caught sight of my reflection in the hall mirror and saw that I had a black eye coming up where I'd struck the doorknob. I had a sudden surge of confidence.

'I'm not pleased either that I've had a nasty accident, Miss Marks, and I have been advised on medical grounds to stay at home. If you have a problem with that you can take it up with... with...' I scrambled around in my mind for the name of the teacher's union I was paying to be a member of.

'The NUT? AHDS? ASCL? The UTU?' asked Miss Marks sarcastically.

'Yes. Them,' I said and put the phone down. I hoped my black eye would turn into a right shiner before I went back to school tomorrow.

We got Rosencrantz ready for school, and I kissed him goodbye at the front door.

'Mummy, why is your eye all black? Did you look through one of those joke telescopes?' he asked.

'Yes, I did,' I lied.

'Wow! Can I try it? Where is it?'

'It's Mr Cohen's from next door. He popped round earlier to play a joke on Mummy,' I said.

'You wouldn't think Mr Cohen is into jokes, he always looks such a bloody misery guts!' said Rosencrantz.

'Rosencrantz, don't be rude!'

'I'm only saying what you said the other day,' said Rosencrantz.

'Well, Mummy shouldn't have said that...'

'Come on son, we'll be late for school,' interrupted Daniel.

They both gave me a kiss and I watched them for a moment, Daniel, and his little doppelgänger walking off, chatting away. My heart was fit to burst with love.

Whilst Daniel walked Rosencrantz round to school, I dug out the *AA Road Atlas* and plotted our course to the mysterious lay-by on the route to Dover. We set off in the car just after eight, picking up Ethel in Catford on the way. There were miles and miles of roadworks along the dual carriageway towards Dover. The digging for the Channel Tunnel terminals was causing chaos. Daniel sat in the front with me, reading the map, and Ethel was in the back. Although she didn't sit back, preferring to peer through the seats and eyeball me in the rearview mirror.

'Put yer foot down, Coco!' she said. It was ten to ten and the van was due to stop in the lay-by at ten.

'Ethel, we're bumper to bumper in this queue,' I said.

'Ain't there a back road?'

'We have to stay on the dual carriageway, because that's where the lorry is stopping,' I said.

Ethel leaned through the seats and honked the horn.

'No, Mum, don't do that,' chided Daniel, pulling her hand away.

'They shouldn't be doin' this, digging tunnels under the Channel,' muttered Ethel darkly. 'They're openin' a Pandora's box. The French will be able to walk to England, and the tunnels'll be flooded with rabid dogs!'

The cars in front began to move and we inched forward. The dual carriageway was reduced to one lane and we were crawling along beside a row of traffic cones. Daniel poked his head out of the passenger window.

'It's okay, it's just up ahead,' he said, pointing past the rows of cars stretching ahead to a lay-by appearing over the brow of the hill. We inched forward some more, and could make out a stationary lorry. The line of cars began to move quicker.

'It's fine, we'll be there in a couple of minutes,' I said, changing up to second gear.

'Me an' Bert go way back, so you let me do the talking,' said Ethel for the fifteenth time that day. "'E's a very reliable bloke. So were 'is homing pidgins, they were always the first back.'

A roadworks van passed in the blocked-off lane beside us, and came to a stop parallel to the lay-by up ahead.

'Tha's Bert! Tha's 'im,' yelled Ethel in my ear, as a balding man with a paunch climbed down from the lorry. At the same time, two blokes in hard hats got out of the roadworks van. I was about to turn off the carriageway into the lay-by, when one of them walked into our lane with a huge stop sign on a pole. He planted it on the ground and I applied the brakes. The other bloke was now shifting the road cones, creating a gap through to the empty lane next to us and blocking off the lane in front.

'Hang on, what's going on here?' said Daniel. The bloke holding the sign then flipped it round to the green 'GO' side, and indicated I drive through the gap into the next lane.

'We're being diverted,' I said, not knowing what to do.

'We can't go, Coco, we'll miss the bloody lay-by!' cried Ethel, leaning through the gap in the front seats.

A car behind honked its horn. The bloke in the hard hat waved at me to move. I wound down my window.

'Sorry, I need to get to that lay-by!' I said, pointing at the lorry. Bert was now unlocking the back.

'GO!' he shouted, waving at me. More cars started to honk behind.

'Don't go, Coco!' squawked Ethel, grabbing my arm through the gap in the seats.

'I've got to go! I'm blocking the road!' I screeched.

'But it's Bert, look, 'e's got the bloody lorry open!' cried Ethel.

There was a muffled clatter as the back door of the lorry whooshed up, and we could see pallets of coloured boxes swathed in shrink wrap. The bloke with the 'GO' sign up ahead was now very angry and yelling, waving his arms. A cacophony of honking was coming from behind.

'Shit!' I shouted.

I put the car in gear and turned into the next lane. The diversion led us across two lanes and through a gap in the central reservation! We emerged in a lane on the opposite side of the road. We stopped parallel to the lay-by at a set of temporary traffic lights, which were red. A giant truck started to cross, piled high with earth.

'Bert, you cheeky bastard!' shouted Ethel in my ear.

She pointed across the central reservation, past the rows of cars to where Bert was sticking a large square of cardboard to the side of the lorry. Printed in marker pen he'd written: **TRACY IRELANDS FOR SALE**.

'Bert told me it was just a trusted few people! I never liked 'im, nor his scrawny diseased pidgins!' Ethel squawked. Four cars and a small van left the queue and turned off the road into the lay-by. 'Do something, Coco! There'll be none left!'

'Will you stop your mother shouting in my ear,' I snapped to a helpless Daniel.

'Coco, yer bloody useless!' cried Ethel.

'What can I do? We're on a dual carriageway! You want me to abandon the car and walk?' I yelled.

People were now getting out of their cars in the lay-by and congregating around the back of the lorry.

'Well, if you won't, I will!' declared Ethel. She opened the car door and jumped out.

'What are you doing, Mum?' yelled Daniel.

Ethel made for the metal barrier of the central reservation. She hitched up her skirt and hooked one leg over.

'Why did you have to go and put that idea in her head?' said Daniel.

'Oh, it's my fault, is it? Ethel, this is a dual carriageway!' I shouted.

'Yer too bloody soft Coco!' she shouted back. 'I survived the Blitz. I can survive crossing a bloody road!'

'Weren't you evacuated to the Lake District?' I'm not too sure why I felt it relevant to contradict her, but she was ignoring me and was now straddling the central reservation, skirt hitched up above her huge grey knickers, now on show to the line of cars behind. A couple of windows wound down and a huge bloke in a white van shouted, 'Nice arse, grandma! You escaped from the funny farm?'

'You shut yer mouth, you fat bastard, I'm Christmas shopping!' shouted Ethel.

The traffic light was still red, and the lorry carrying dirt had nearly cleared the lane in front.

'Go and get her, Daniel, the lights are going to change,' I said.

He jumped out of the car and went round to grab Ethel but she managed to get her other leg over the central reservation and climb down on the other side. She dashed between the stationary cars and into the lay-by. Fifteen or twenty people were now congregating around the back of the lorry, waving cash at Bert.

'Come on, Danny! There's gonna be none left for little Rosencrantz!' called Ethel.

Daniel was now over the central reservation and running around the cars to join her in the lay-by.

Seized with a crazed fear of losing out, I unclipped my seat belt and abandoned the car, leaping over the central reservation to join them. Ignoring the fat bloke behind who was still laughing.

There was an undignified tussle at the rear of the lorry. People were pushing and shoving, and Ethel was squaring up to a tiny little woman with fuzzy grey hair. In the interior of the lorry was a fast-dwindling pile of Tracy Islands. Ethel fought her way through and clambered up into the lorry, smearing what looked like engine oil down the front of her coat. Before Bert could stop her, she seized one of the last boxed Tracy Islands.

'Coco, 'ere, I've got one,' she shouted, throwing it to me at the back of the crowd. Luckily I caught it.

'Ethel, get down,' said Bert.

''Ow much, Bert?' she asked.

'Sixty,' said Bert, who was taking fistfuls of cash in one hand and handing out the last few Tracy Island boxes with the other.

'Sixty quid, Bert? Ain't they in the shops for about thirty?' shouted Ethel. He reached the last of the Tracy Islands, and then the wooden pallet was empty. I clutched the Tracy Island box to my chest.

'It's sixty quid, Ethel. I could get skinned alive for doin' this!' said Bert.

'I've got fifty-five 'ere, Bert, take it or leave it,' announced Ethel, putting her hand in her coat and pulling out a bundle of notes.

'The RRP is £34.99,' shouted the old lady with the fuzzy hair, 'but I'll pay sixty-five!'

'It'll be RIP for you if you don't keep yer trap shut!' snarled Ethel.

'I'll pay seventy!' yelled another lady in a red woolly hat.

'Seventy-five,' chimed a young couple in matching winter coats.

'Bert. You owe me,' frowned Ethel.

Bert wiped his face, looked at the cash Ethel was holding out, then took it.

'We got one, we got one!!!' said Daniel, turning to me with a grin.

'The littlun's gonna be made up! 'E's gonna get a Tracy bloody Island on Christmas Day! Only the best for my grandson!' grinned Ethel as Bert helped her down from the back of the lorry.

By now the lights had changed to green. There was crazed honking and the road workers were screaming at us to get back into our car, which had three doors open and the engine running. We didn't care though. We had Tracy Island!!

When we finally got back home, we sat round the kitchen table with a pot of tea and some fruit cake.

'You did well, Ethel. Thank you,' I said as we stared at Tracy Island in the middle of the table. The box was so colourful. I wiped away a tear.

'Rosencrantz is going to be thrilled,' said Daniel, his bottom lip trembling.

Ethel's face crumpled in tears and she got up.

'Well, I can't 'ang around 'ere gas-bagging', I'd best be off. Don't get up Coco, love.'

We all composed ourselves, feeling a bit embarrassed.

'Would you like us to get you a taxi, Ethel?' I asked.

'Gawd no, love, I'll get the bus.'

'Thank you, Ethel. I know we don't...'

'Save yer breath for blowin' out candles, love. Where Rosencrantz is concerned I think we're in agreement,' she smiled.

She patted me on the shoulder and then Daniel showed her to the front door. When he came back he grabbed my hand and gave it a squeeze.

'It looks like Thunderbirds are go!' he smiled.

WEDNESDAY 16TH DECEMBER

We had a few too many celebratory drinks last night, so when I woke up I was hungover and my black eye was very pronounced. To quote Rosencrantz, I looked like I'd been looking through Mr Cohen's joke telescope again. I debated leaving my face bare, but decided to slap on some foundation, otherwise the kids in my class wouldn't let me hear the end of it.

I arrived in the staff car park and checked my reflection in the rear-view mirror. I realised I should have put on some lipstick and eyeliner. I was a rather odd, pale colour. The Ripper must have seen me arrive because he was waiting by the school entrance when I reached it. His cold blue eyes were arctic.

'Mrs Pinchard. A word. In my office,' he snapped.

I followed him inside, past Miss Marks sitting at her desk with a smirk playing across her pointed face. I'd never been in The Ripper's office before. It was vast and rather bare. A couple of certificates dotted the walls, and on a bookshelf there were a few spider plants which looked like they'd been read their last rites. I could hear muffled shrieks from the playground outside, but the windows had blinds drawn against the weak December sun.

He motioned for me to sit at his large, polished wood desk. He sat opposite and stared at me. His eyes seemed to see into my head, poking around inappropriately at the folds of my grey matter.

'You informed Miss Marks yesterday that you were ill,' he said, finally.

'Yes. I had a concussion... Is it *a concussion* or just *concussion?*'

He shrugged. 'You're the English teacher, Mrs Pinchard.'

'I had concussion, Mr Sutcliffe,' I said, wishing I hadn't covered up my black eye. I looked like an odd-coloured liar.

'A concussion at home?' he asked.

'Of course, where else would I be concussed?'

'I don't know. A car accident? Your car looks fine though. Did you go to hospital?'

'No.'

'Then how did you know you had concussion?' he asked. I paused.

'I was under the impression I only need to provide you with a detailed sick note after my third day of absence?' I said.

'Of course,' he smiled. 'I'm just checking you're okay. I know that concussion can make one forgetful.'

'No, I'm fine. Apart from the grammatical mistake re 'a concussion' or 'concussion'.'

I was babbling now. He opened his drawer and pulled out a copy of *The Sun*. A page had been marked with a yellow post-it. He opened it, and placed the newspaper on the polished desk in front of me. The headline read: **TRACY**

ISLAND MANIA! He tapped at a picture with his manicured hand.

'This woman looks a lot like you, Mrs Pinchard,' he said.

I looked down in horror at the double-page spread. Pictures from around the country showed empty shelves in toyshops, fights breaking out in queues at the till, and it included a series of photos taken yesterday at the lay-by. I leaned into the picture: tiny images of me, Daniel and Ethel could be made out amongst the throng at the back of the lorry. Who'd been taking photos? A lurking journalist? Miss Marks?

'Do you think so?' I said. 'That photo is a little blurred...'

'And that's your husband, yes?'

'Um, is it? As I said, it's very blurred...'

'This is a very clear picture of your husband, Mrs Pinchard. I have met him twice and I can recognise him. So?'

'I suppose it *could* be him. Although, what he was doing at that lay-by...'

'It could be him? If so, who would this woman be he's got his arm around, if it wasn't you?'

'Ooh, I'm going to have words with him when I get home!' I grinned manically. I started to sweat.

'This is not the time to joke!' he said, slamming his hand down on the polished wood, making me jump.

Say something normal! a voice screamed in my head. But I just sat there and looked guilty. The Ripper swallowed and sat back in his chair. The silence was deafening.

'Was the Christingle assembly a success?' I chirruped eventually.

'Was the Christingle assembly a success, *WAS THE CHRISTINGLE ASSEMBLY A SUCCESS*?' he roared.

'Is that a yes?' I said.

The Ripper went a funny shade of purple and tried to compose himself.

'Your form was unsupervised, and started throwing Christingle oranges at the choir,' he growled. 'They changed the words from 'Walking In A Winter Wonderland' to 'Wanking In A Winter Wonderland' and one boy asked the Lady Mayoress to *show him her fanny.*'

'And what did she do?' I heard myself ask. Why couldn't I keep my mouth shut?

'Well, she didn't, OBVIOUSLY, MRS PINCHARD!' shouted The Ripper, losing it again. He stood up and thumped his desk.

'SO I'LL ASK YOU AGAIN. WHERE WERE YOU YESTERDAY?'

I reacted like a naughty year eight pupil caught smoking behind the bike sheds: I sang like a canary. I blurted out that I had done what any mother would have done, and I had gone to track down a Tracy Island toy for Christmas. I waited to hear that I was sacked but...

'You've got a Tracy Island?' he said sharply.

'Yes.'

'A genuine one?'

'Yes.'

He stood and went to the window. He lifted the blind for a moment, then let it drop.

'Look, Mrs Pinchard,' he said evenly. 'I also have a son. A son I rarely see due to the pressures of being a headmaster.'

'So you must understand, Headmaster,' I pleaded.

He was composed now. He came and sat back at his desk. He opened his desk drawer and pulled out a file. I noticed it had my name on the front.

'I'm having to make some difficult decisions about St

Dukes. We're experiencing budget cuts and I have to make a teacher redundant.'

'I thought Miss Bruce was retiring?'

'Only if she decides to... If not, I have to make a tough decision. One teacher will be getting a P45 for Christmas.'

'Are you threatening me?' I frowned.

'No, no, no,' he said as if I were a silly little girl. 'You are an able teacher, popular with pupils. But, I have a great deal of able teachers who are just as popular, and when I make my decision I have to be fair. I have to look at things like attendance records, and of course you are one of our newest staff members. So...' He tapped the file against his teeth.

'So?' I asked.

He pulled the newspaper toward him and twisted it round.

'So I wish I'd known about those Tracy Islands. Getting one for Christmas would make my son happy, my wife happy, and, naturally, me happy. And when I'm happy I'm a much more reasonable Headmaster,' he said. He was now calm, collected. Then the penny dropped.

'You want me to give you the Tracy Island?' I said. He kept staring at me. 'No. No, NO, I'm sorry, Headmaster. This is my son's Christmas present. Please. No...'

He kept staring at me with his cold eyes. I jumped when the bell rang to signal morning registration. Miss Marks knocked and came in.

'Mr Sutcliffe, I've got the Lady Mayoress on the phone, asking about the written apology?'

'Yes, thank you, Miss Marks. I was just discussing the pupil in question with Mrs Pinchard.' He turned his attention back to me. 'I'll need that written apology on my desk by lunchtime, and think carefully about what we discussed.'

I nodded and tried to compose myself. Picking up my bag I left his office.

I had to give my class a dressing down when what I really wanted was to tell them well done for trashing The Ripper's Christingle assembly. When morning break came round I went to the ladies loos near the domestic science block, which are always empty. I locked myself in a cubicle and had a good cry. I didn't hear anyone come in, and was surprised when there was a knock on the cubicle door. I froze. The knock came again.

'Yes?' I said.

'Mrs Pinchard, is that you? Are you all right?' asked Miss Rolincova in her Slovak accent.

'Yes, I'm fine, thank you,' I said.

There was a pause.

'You don't sound fine, you are crying your head off.'

Bloody woman, I thought, *bugger off.*

'No I'm fine, really,' I insisted.

'There is much chatterings in the staffroom about you pretending to be sick from work yesterday. And they are all passing round a newspaper with a picture of you in it.'

I wiped my eyes, undid the lock, and opened the door. Miss Rolincova was perched on the line of sinks. She offered me a tissue.

'Thanks,' I said, taking the tissue and blowing my nose. 'So everybody knows?'

She nodded. 'They say The Ripper caught you bonking off.'

'It's bunking – bunking off,' I said. 'And yes, I was caught.'

'I have never properly introduced myself. I'm Marika,' she said smiling.

'I'm Coco.' She nodded and we shook hands. 'What else are they saying?' I asked.

'Who cares what else they're saying. That old crone who eats perished fruit is, as usual, being a bitch, and Mr Gutteridge, who smells like urine, was agreeing you should be given the sack. What is this sack? Some kind of bag?'

'It means I'll be fired. I'll lose my job,' I said.

'Ah, sorry.... Fuck. My English, I feel it will never get better.'

'You speak really good English,' I told her, wiping my eyes with the tissue.

'My God, woman!' she cried.

'What?' I said, peering into the mirror. 'Oh...'

My tears had uncovered my black eye. I told her about slipping over on a pile of exercise books. She pulled a little pencil case out of her handbag, made me wash my face, then gently she re-applied my make-up. I couldn't help but stare at her as she worked. She has a kind face, amazing cheekbones and beautiful long dark hair. She grinned when she was finished and turned me to face the mirrors.

'Wow,' I said, admiring her handiwork.

'How do you say? Army paint?'

'War paint,' I laughed.

Marika nodded and smiled. 'Now you can face the battle,' she said.

The bell rang out as if it had heard us.

'What are you doing for lunch?' I asked. 'I can't face the staffroom today. You fancy coming to the caff round the corner? My treat.'

She hesitated. 'Okay, yes.'

We agreed to meet outside the staffroom, and we dashed off to our respective classes. I was intrigued to go out for lunch with Marika. I'd been teaching at St Dukes for nearly four months, and she was the first person I felt like I'd connected with. I wonder if she felt the same, or was she just taking pity on me?

When lunch came round I was nervous. Marika was waiting for me outside the staffroom in her winter coat. As we walked out of school The Ripper was leaning over Miss Marks's desk and in conversation. He looked up at me.

'Thank you for the note of apology, Mrs Pinchard. Do think carefully about what I said.' His eyes bored into mine and I shivered.

Outside it had started to snow, so we took my car the short way to the Italian café. The windows were steamed up, and a row of Christmas lights gave the mist a multi-coloured hue. I ordered lasagne, a green salad, and a large glass of red wine. Marika spent a long time studying the menu and settled on a green salad and a glass of tap water.

'Aren't you very hungry?' I asked. She shrugged. 'You're slimming?'

'Yes,' she said unconvincingly.

When our food arrived my lasagne was thankfully enormous, so I offloaded a quarter onto Marika, saying that if she didn't help me it would end up in the bin. We ate quickly and when the plates were cleared away I ordered a coffee and offered her a cigarette. There was a copy of *The Sun* on the next table and I grabbed it to have a proper look. I told Marika about everything that had happened. She listened attentively. When I finished she was silent. She could see I was uncomfortable and looked back down at the newspaper.

'Look at this old lady! You can see her knickers when she climbs over this... What do you call this barrier?'

'The central reservation. That's Daniel's mother. My mother-in-law,' I explained.

'She looks a little crazy.'

'You don't know the half of it,' I said. I lit up another cigarette and offered another to Marika. 'So how do you get to work?' I asked.

'The tube train, on the red line from Epping.'

'You're living out in Epping? That's miles away!'

'I have to get the bus to Epping tube and then I change at Oxford Circus to get up here.'

'But that must take you ages?'

'Two hours, sometimes two and half...'

She smiled and flicked the ash from her cigarette.

'I'm happy to be here though. It's hard to get a work permit for England, and teachers at home make nothing.'

'Did you always want to be a teacher?' I asked.

'I like kids, well, I thought I did, but the past four months at St Dukes have made me think again. What about you?' she asked.

'I had, have... no, had dreams of being a writer but life seems to have got in the way. I had my son four years ago, and then my parents died, leaving me a business which was bankrupt. I had to get serious. I thought teaching English would be bearable, but... St Dukes is...' I trailed off.

'No wonder they call it St Puke's,' grinned Marika.

I laughed too, adding, 'I think you're the first sane person I've met there.'

'Mr Wednesday, the Art teacher, has been kind,' said Marika.

'Are you two...?' I asked.

'No. He is just a friend,' said Marika.

'He's rather gorgeous too, but he seems to spend the whole time in his art room and then leaves when the bell goes. Is he married? Gay?'

'I don't think he is married. And I have never met a gay man, so I wouldn't know,' shrugged Marika.

'You've never met a gay man?' I exclaimed.

Marika shook her head.

'But we're in London! Gay men are everywhere!'

'In Slovakia things like that are kept quiet. It's a beautiful country but very... religious. Oh, I must sound like such a villager!'

'No. I was just teasing. In fact, thanks,' I said.

'For what?'

'Coming to lunch, listening...'

Marika grinned.

'What do you think I should do about The Ripper?' I added.

'I'd sell him the toy for a big profit,' she said, exhaling cigarette smoke out of the corner of her mouth.

'But Rosencrantz really, really wants Tracy Island for Christmas.'

'But this is your job, Coco. Your source of income to live. Can't you get your son a toy plane or a boat?'

'You don't understand,' I sighed.

'I don't think you understand, Coco. There is a recession on, you have a job and you are willing to risk it all for a child's toy? Are material things that important?' When she put it like that I couldn't argue. 'I'm sorry if I am direct, but I am direct with all my friends,' she added.

'Do you want to be friends?' I said.

'Yes, you just passed the interview.'

'Oh,' I said.

'I'm joking,' she grinned. 'You are the first person in England I have been to lunch with.'

'How long have you been in England?'

'Five months,' she said.

As we drove back to school I took stock of everything. I realised just how lucky I was.

❄

When I got home, and whilst Rosencrantz was in the living room watching *Noddy's Adventures in Toyland,* I told Daniel what had transpired at school.

'I'll knock his bloody block off! What a twat!' said Daniel, reaching for his coat on the back of his chair.

'Yes, thank you. That will solve all our problems, you punching my boss.'

'I'm not having him blackmailing my wife!' he said, pulling on his coat.

'This is how men run the world.' I rolled my eyes. 'Smacking each other about because they don't like what they hear.'

'Where does he live?'

'High Barnet.'

'Oh,' said Daniel, looking at the heavy snow falling outside the kitchen window.

'Oh! The romance,' I said. 'No, Marika is right, I should just sell him the toy at a profit.'

'That's giving in!'

'Don't you worry, I'll find a way to get back at him.'

'But what about Rosencrantz? He's *desperate* for Tracy Island. It's the only thing he wants for Christmas,' said Daniel.

On cue Rosencrantz came bursting into the kitchen.

'Mummy! Daddy! Can I have a Bumpy Dog for Christmas?' he asked breathlessly.

'A Bumpy Dog?' I said.

'Yes, like the one Noddy has got. He's white and small and a bit bumpy, but I could train him!'

Daniel looked at me.

'Pleeeeeease Mummy and Daddy, can I have a Bumpy Dog for Christmas?' he said, jiggling on the spot in anticipation.

'What about Tracy Island?' asked Daniel.

Rosencrantz screwed up his face in concentration and put his hand down the front of his trousers.

'You don't need to fiddle with yourself,' I said.

'Sorry, Mummy, it helps me think. Daddy does it too.'

'No I don't,' said Daniel quickly.

'I think,' said Rosencrantz, 'that forty-three percent of me wants a Tracy Island, but a massive four hundred percent of me wants a Bumpy Dog.'

'But you've already written to Father Christmas,' Daniel reminded him. 'Ow!' he added as I kicked him under the table.

'The secretary at my school knows everyone's number. What if I got her to fax the North Pole, saying you've changed your mind and you want a Bumpy Dog?' I suggested.

'Does Father Christmas have a fax machine?' wondered Daniel.

'YES, he does,' I said, rounding on him. 'He's got flying reindeer, so it goes without saying he's got a fax machine.'

Rosencrantz was looking at us seriously. 'So you can ask her, on tomorrow, if she can fax Father Christmas so he can get me a Bumpy Dog?'

'Yes,' I said.

'Not *too* bumpy though, Mummy. I wouldn't want it to knock Nan over.'

'Of course,' I said.

Rosencrantz seemed satisfied and went back to the living room.

'So as well as not giving him Tracy Island, we're now promising him a dog?' said Daniel.

We were quiet for a moment; Daniel put his hand down his trousers deep in thought.

'Not you too! Leave it alone!' I snapped.

THURSDAY 17TH DECEMBER

I got to school early this morning and asked to see The Ripper in his office. Miss Marks showed me through. He was eating Rice Krispies at his desk with a huge napkin tucked into the collar of his shirt.

'Ah, Mrs Pinchard,' he said, wiping his mouth and indicating the seat opposite.

I sat and waited for Miss Marks to bugger off. When she'd gone, I took Tracy Island out of a carrier bag, and placed it carefully on the desk in front of him.

A hush seemed to descend on the room, broken by the occasional snap, crackle, and pop from his cereal.

He pushed the bowl to one side and pulled out a pair of reading glasses. He polished them slowly, then popped them on and began to peer at the box, turning it over. A clock ticked loudly. I felt like I was on the *Antiques Roadshow* and he was going to tell me what a marvellous find it was.

'I'm selling it to you for a hundred pounds,' I said.

Daniel and I had agreed that The Ripper was on a good

salary and the bastard could at least cover all of our Christmas booze, plus crackers and a new set of fairy lights.

'And that's what you paid for it, Mrs Pinchard? Tracy Island retails at £34.99,' said The Ripper, looking at me over the top of his glasses.

'You saw the people at the back of that van, Headmaster. The wild-eyed hysteria. The closer we get to Christmas, the more valuable these become,' I said.

'So it will cost me almost three times as much?'

'Yes, and during January I won't be doing playground duty either.'

He raised his eyebrows and sat back.

'Are you in a position to negotiate?' he said.

I noticed beside his phone there was a picture of The Ripper with his family. His wife was small and quite ferocious-looking. His son had an unfortunate mix of their genes. I went to pick up the box. He put his hand on mine.

'No, hang on, I'm sure something can be arranged,' he said. I shivered and pulled my hand away.

I left his office with five crisp twenty-pound notes and a promise I wouldn't have to stand in the cold during January blowing a whistle. I ran to the toilets and thought I was going to be sick. My heart was pounding. That man terrified me. I ran the tap and splashed cold water on my face. I felt complete despair at losing Rosencrantz's Christmas present, but I would keep my job.

Right now, if I could get away with it, I could have quite happily killed The Ripper.

FRIDAY 18TH DECEMBER

The kids were unbearable at school today, and who could blame them? Christmas was now tantalisingly close. I couldn't believe we had to come back next week on Monday and Tuesday before the Christmas holidays began.

Like politics, a week is a long time at St Dukes, and the teaching staff were more concerned about a pending redundancy. Whispers were going round about who it would be, and Miss Bruce was getting a kick out of knowing it wasn't her. She sat watching everyone from a ripped armchair under the window, chomping on a blackened banana.

Marika came up to me by the tea urn, and asked if I was okay. I said that Daniel was at home, working the phone and trying to get hold of another Tracy Island.

'What about you? You look like you haven't slept a wink!' I said, noticing how exhausted she was with dark circles under her eyes. 'I'm sure you're safe from the redundancy,' I added hopefully.

'It's not that. My electricity has stopped working,' she said quietly.

'Marika, it went down to minus five last night!' I cried.

'I know.'

'Has the circuit breaker tripped?'

'My landlord hasn't paid the bill,' she said.

Marika went on to say that she hadn't got a phone, so I insisted she came back home with me at lunch time to use ours and get it sorted.

When we came through the front door, Daniel was lolling on the sofa, still in his dressing gown, watching *Sons and Daughters.*

'Cokes, you didn't tell me you were coming back,' he yelped, leaping up, smoothing down his hair, and making sure nothing was hanging out of the gap in his pyjama bottoms. I introduced him to Marika.

'Hello,' he smiled.

'What have you found out about Tracy Island?' I asked.

'Um, I've got some good leads,' he said.

'Like what?' I probed, taking in his breakfast things which were still on the coffee table.

'I think I'll go and, er, get dressed... I don't normally loll around watching Australian soaps all day,' he said before bolting upstairs.

'He should be organising Christmas, not watching bloody crap on TV,' I grumbled when he'd gone.

We'd stopped off on the way back and bought jacket potatoes, and we sat on the sofa eating them out of the containers.

'Does he have a job?' asked Marika, through a mouthful of potato.

'Yes, he writes music for pantomimes and plays. He's a composer.'

'Is he writing something now?'

'No, he finished for Christmas,' I said.

We chewed for a moment.

'When does he start again?' asked Marika.

'I'm... not sure, he's looking for work,' I said.

Marika looked at me for a moment and went to say more, but I changed the subject and phoned the electricity board. I found out that Marika's landlord owed £195. Marika paled when she heard that.

'My rent is supposed to be all-inclusive!' she said.

I asked her if she could pay it over the phone with her credit card and then get the money back from her landlord, but she said she couldn't afford it. I then offered to pay, but she wasn't having any of that. I put the phone down and there was an awkward moment broken by the front door bell.

I went to answer it, and came back through into the living room with my best friend, Chris. Marika looked a little shocked when she saw what he was wearing: a floor-length yellow and sky blue tartan winter coat and Ray-Bans.

'Just call me Mother Christmas!' he said, waving a piece of paper and handing it to me with a flourish.

'What's this?' I asked, taking it from him.

'It's a distribution list!'

'What?'

'Dad gets daily print-outs for his catering business. You know, when he's got merchandise coming in at the docks, blah blah blah.'

'Why would I want to know about what's arriving for your dad's catering business?' I asked.

'Daniel rang me and told me you were looking for a Tracy Island. So I asked my father to pull a few favours with the freight import companies, and I can tell you that there are two thousand Tracy Islands due to dock in Portsmouth later today!'

'Two thousand?' I gasped, scanning the paper he'd given me.

'They're for the whole country, Cokes. But the good news is that Hamleys toy shop in Regent Street is scheduled to receive two hundred tomorrow morning. They open at nine.'

'Oh Chris!' I said, hugging him.

Marika stood shyly by the sofa in her smart work suit and stockinged feet.

'Sorry! Marika, meet Chris,' I added, letting him go.

'Are you a social worker?' asked Chris, taking in her off-the-peg work suit and shaking her hand.

'No. I'm a science teacher,' said Marika.

'What's that accent?' asked Chris.

'Slovak,' said Marika.

'You've got gorgeous cheekbones! And your hair is to die for!' he cried.

He unbuttoned his coat and underneath was wearing a denim three–piece-suit with sliver buttons and a red necktie. He reached into a pocket and pulled out a roll of fifty-pound notes.

'I also wanted to give you this, Cokes, to add to Rosencrantz's building society account in my capacity as godfather,' said Chris, peeling four fifties off and handing them to me. 'It's from me and Benji. Benji is my new boyfriend,' he added to Marika. She nodded, still rather shocked at the encounter.

'Have you seen *Cats?*' asked Chris.

'Yes. I live above a Chinese restaurant and cats visit the rubbish bins all night,' said Marika dourly. Chris looked thrown.

'No, I meant Andrew Lloyd Webber's *Cats* – in the West End. Benji, my new boyfriend, he plays Rum Tum Tugger, the arrogant Tom... And he gets on like a house on fire with Elaine Paige. He's promised he'll arrange for me to meet her. She's apparently very tiny, Elaine. Benji reckons she could fit through my cat flap, which is quite ironic, don't you think?'

Marika looked totally confused.

'Look, Chris, we've got to get back to work. Thanks so much for the Tracy Island list and the money for Rosencrantz,' I said.

'And you'd best get down to Hamleys early tomorrow, Cokes. Dad says loads of people have been told about this,' added Chris.

Daniel came back downstairs, now dressed.

'Hi Chris,' he said.

'Hi Daniel. What happened in *Sons and Daughters* today?'

'I don't know. I didn't see it all,' said Daniel defensively.

'Chris has found out Hamleys is getting two hundred Tracy Islands tomorrow,' I enthused, 'And he's given Rosencrantz two hundred pounds for his building society account.'

'Thank you,' said Daniel, although he didn't seem pleased. 'Nice suit,' he added. 'I saw a guy wearing one just like it when I went out yesterday.'

'Where?' asked Chris.

'Marylebone High Street. He was pushing a Christmas tree along in a wheelbarrow.'

Chris looked annoyed.

'Bugger! I knew my tailor was a lying bastard as well as a perv. I can cope with being felt up when he measures my inside leg, but lying about this suit being an original. I need to have words... Right, I'd best be off, Cokes. Lovely to meet you Marika.' Chris gave a surprised Marika a kiss, buttoned up his coat and left.

'In case you hadn't realised, Marika, that was your first encounter with a gay man,' I said.

Marika laughed and Daniel scowled and went off upstairs.

'Did you order a turkey? And what about a tree?' I yelled up, as he took the stairs two at a time.

'I will,' he shouted.

'And we're going to Hamleys in the morning, early. So ring Ethel and ask if she can come and stay tonight so she can be with Rosencrantz tomorrow.'

'Yes!' he shouted moodily.

Marika and I stood awkwardly in silence for a moment in the hall. Her eyes flickered to the two hundred quid I was holding. I stuffed it in my pocket and we made our way back to school.

SATURDAY 19TH DECEMBER

When we left the house this morning at six o'clock it was pitch black outside and the orange light from the street lamps could barely make it through the freezing fog.

'Now don't be shy about pushing people, and if someone falls over in the stampede don't help 'em up,' said Ethel, handing us a flask of tea at the front door. 'Particularly you, Coco. Yer far too nice fer yer own good.'

'I'm nice too,' protested Daniel.

'No, yer like me, son,' said Ethel.

'I don't know when we'll be back,' I told her.

'I can be 'ere all day. Rosencrantz will be fine, love. Just bring 'im back Tracy Island,' said Ethel.

We took a taxi and arrived on Regent Street at quarter past six. I thought we'd be ridiculously early, but when we rounded the crossroads at Oxford Street, I could see crash barriers had been erected around the entrance to Hamleys and a substantial number of people were already waiting. I joined the back of the queue, whilst Daniel went along to count how many were in front of us.

'We're one hundred and ninety-eighth,' he said when he came back.

'It's going to be close then,' I groaned.

Over the next couple of hours, we drank our tea and stamped our feet to try and keep warm. As it started to get light, the canopy of Christmas lights above us flicked off and the line continued to grow, snaking back past us and vanishing round the curve of Regent Street. An aggressive silence hung over everything, punctuated by a BBC television news crew moving past the line to document the Tracy Island mania. At one point they stopped in front of us, and a bright light came on above the camera, illuminating a windswept-looking couple. They perked up when they realised they would be on telly, saying they'd driven down from Norfolk at two o'clock this morning in the hope of getting a Tracy Island for their son, who is in a wheelchair. I felt rather guilty about the thoughts I'd had of pushing them to the ground and walking over them both. Then the BBC television crew moved past, and the couple from Norfolk were silent.

At quarter to nine, it was light with a thin fog still hanging in the air. I noticed a little old man working his way down the line, holding a pile of leaflets. At first I thought that he was a born again Christian, or one of the touts for open-top bus journeys, but I noticed that almost everyone he stopped beside was rooting around for spare change and buying a leaflet. I told Daniel to keep our place, hoisted myself over the barrier and went down to him.

'What's that you're selling?' I asked.

'Maps, of the inside of Hamleys,' he said. He had on fingerless gloves and an old winter coat. His nose and ears were sprouting tufts of grey hair.

'How much?' I said.

I saw that the maps were hand-drawn, and had been photocopied badly.

'A pound,' he replied.

'*A pound*?'

'There's seven floors in Hamleys. Do you know where the Tracy Islands are going to be?' he demanded.

'No. Do you?'

'No,' he admitted. 'But with this map you'll find 'em quicker, won't you love?'

I agreed he had a point and forked out a quid. I took the map back to Daniel. We went into a huddle and pored over it, deciding that Tracy Island would probably be on 'Boys' Toys' on the fourth floor, or 'Boxed Games' on the third, or, ideally, that they'd have piled them up by the front door.

'The latter makes sense, surely?' I said.

'Yeah, we're all here for the same thing!' said Daniel.

I felt a tap on my shoulder. I turned, and there was a tiny woman behind us with an immaculate brown hair in a bowl cut, which made her head look like a polished conker.

'This is the queue for Hamleys?' she asked.

'Yes. You're one-hundred-and-ninety-ninth,' I said. The woman looked confused. 'For the Tracy Islands,' I added. 'There's only two hundred, apparently.'

'Don't tell her that,' hissed Daniel through his teeth.

'No, I'm here to buy the Sylvanian Families Treehouse,' she said.

'Do you have children or grandchildren?' I asked.

'Neither. I thought the Sylvanian Families would be nice company to have in the house, you know, over Christmas. They're much easier to keep than live animals. Believe me, I know. I had a hamster. So what's Tracy Island?'

Daniel gave me a look. I gave him a look back to say this

woman was obviously a bit mad, and so it was okay to tell her. Then I briefly explained about Tracy Island mania.

'But there're plenty of Sylvanian Family Treehouses? I don't want to spend Christmas alone again,' she asked anxiously.

'I'm sure they're plenty,' I said, smiling.

She smiled sweetly back. Suddenly a ripple of voices ran through the queue and then, Hamleys was open! The line began to surge forward. I hooked my handbag over both arms and got ready to shop. The queue slowed and I could feel a push from behind.

'It's not me, dear,' said the little lady. 'They're pushing from the back.'

'Don't crowd us!' I snapped at the people behind, but they returned a determined stare.

As we moved past the windows of Hamleys, towards the main entrance, there was a puppet of Lady Penelope behind the glass in her elegant pink drawing room with a cigarette in a holder. Parker stood to one side, proffering an ashtray. *Who'd have thought kids would be still be interested in all this in 1992, puppets on strings?* I thought.

The queue surged forward again, and we were at the door! Someone dressed as a giant teddy bear came out of the entrance with a man in a policeman's outfit. The man from Norfolk barged inside, knocking the huge teddy bear over, blocking our path. The woman from Norfolk took no notice and managed to scoot round him and through the door as the policeman got the bear half up, but the bear was too heavy and fell back down pulling the policeman with him.

'Why have they put bloody costume characters here?' I shrieked. They were now blocking the doorway. 'Oi, Plod and Bear, move your arses!'

I went to step over them, but the policeman grabbed me by the arm. Daniel managed to leap over them and get inside.

'Hey! Get off,' I said.

'Madam, you need to cool it,' said the policeman.

'I don't need some out-of-work actor in a stupid policeman's costume telling me what to do,' I snapped.

The policeman kept his grip on my arm and used the other hand to pull out his ID.

'Ah...' I said, reading that he was indeed a real policeman.

'Yes, ah,' he said.

'I'm very sorry,' I apologised and tried to pull away.

'Not so fast, madam,' he said.

The giant teddy bear had now righted himself and people were streaming past. I pulled harder, but the policeman held on to my sleeve. People were swarming past either side, bashing us back and forward in a little dance.

'Let me go!' I cried.

'Not until you calm down,' he said, red in the face.

A very tall man rushed past, smashing his shoulder into the back of the policeman's helmet. It slid forward over his eyes. I managed to yank my arm away, and I ran for it into Hamleys.

There was chaos: people were surging and crowding through the shop, which was packed with Christmas toys, piled high, lights winking and blinking.

'Coco!' I heard Daniel shout.

I looked round and saw him being carried upwards on an escalator packed with people. He mouthed something.

'What?' I yelled.

He mouthed again. I still didn't understand. He rolled his eyes.

'Basement!' he shouted.

'They're in the basement?'

He nodded, and then vanished as the escalator took him up and out of sight. I spied a neon arrow on the wall where the basement stairs led down. The crowd had heard Daniel and headed that way too. I felt a small, strong arm push me out of the way. It was the little Sylvanian Families lady who had been behind us in the line.

'What are you pushing for? I thought you wanted a Treehouse?' I said.

But she was gone, towards the neon arrow. I followed and the stairs took us all round twice before we were in the huge electronics department in the basement. The crowd fanned out.

'Where are they?'

'Tracy Island?'

'Where have you got them?' people were shouting.

I ran blindly to one corner, but there was just a rack of Game Boys and posters. I felt like I was on *The Crystal Maze*.

'The Tracy Island toys are on the fourth floor!' said a harassed sales assistant, cupping her hands around her mouth. Half of the people on the shop floor surged towards the stairs, and the half on my side went to the lift. A big man stabbed at the button, and we waited for a minute until the lift doors opened with a ping. Twenty people piled in, and there was shouting and pushing as the remaining few tried to squeeze behind us.

'Get out of the way, the door won't close,' shrilled a highly-strung female voice. I realised a moment later it was me.

The people refused to budge until the little Sylvanian Families woman gave the three people who had their feet in the lift door a hard shove. With no obstruction, the lift doors closed and we began to move up. A mirror on one side displayed our wild faces. A woman with long mousy hair blew a tendril away from her face and looked as if she were going to cry. The lift slowed and I braced myself.

The doors opened and we were off again. Shouting out, 'Where are they?' we zigzagged through shelves until, at the back, we saw a big blown-up poster for Tracy Island, and below it, a dwindling pile of boxes. I lunged forward, shoving people out of my way. Someone was standing on the back of my maxi-length coat and I couldn't move forward, so I sloughed it off like a snakeskin and kept moving.

Finally I made it to the front and there were three left. Two hands went out and grabbed two of the boxes, and I got the last one! I got it! I clutched it tight to my chest and hurried to the till to pay.

A sales assistant stood there, dumbfounded at the crazy sweaty people. She wanted to take the box from me to scan the barcode, but I wasn't having any of that. Nor would I let her put it in a bag for me. She gave me a receipt and a carrier bag, and I carefully put my Tracy Island box inside. Then I remembered I didn't have my coat. I found it in the centre of the shop floor, covered in mucky footprints. I put the bag down on the floor, and bent down to pick up my coat. Then the little old Sylvanian Families lady whooshed over and crashed into me, dropping the carrier bag she'd been clutching.

'I'm terribly sorry,' she said, then, giving me a twinkly little smile, she picked up her bag and scuttled off.

I finally found Daniel outside Hamleys. He was lying in the back of an ambulance. His shoe and sock were off and the ankle on his left foot was twice its normal size. A rather brusque middle-aged nurse was bandaging it up.

'I fell, Cokes,' he whimpered. 'I tripped over a display of Scottish Barbie dolls and went tumbling down the escalator.'

'He's lucky he didn't break his neck,' said the nurse. 'This isn't what Christmas is about! I think you're going to have to go to hospital and get that looked at. It's a bad sprain.'

Daniel sat back and took a deep breath.

'This will cheer you up. I got the last one!' I said, holding up the plastic bag with a grin. I opened it and pulled out... A SYLVANIAN FAMILIES TREEHOUSE!

'What the FUCK!' I shouted. The nurse looked horrified.

'Have you been drinking?' she asked.

'No, I've been conned!' I looked in the bag in disbelief. I was *sure* I'd picked up a Tracy Island. Then I remembered... The little old Sylvanian Families lady... she'd bashed into me.

'That bitch must have switched it!' I shouted.

There was a silence from Daniel and the nurse, and then a policeman appeared – the one who had grabbed my sleeve.

'Right, that's it! You, OUT!' cried the nurse.

'Causing trouble again, *madam?*' the policeman said.

I didn't wait to find out what would happen next. I ran for it. I steamed down Regent Street, through crowds of Christmas shoppers. I didn't stop until I rounded the corner to Oxford Circus. I looked back. No one was following.

The house was warm when I got in. I followed the sound of voices and laughter through to the living room. A fire had been lit, and Rosencrantz was standing in front of the television. Sitting on the sofa were Ethel, Chris and Benji. Chris's new boyfriend was dark-haired, lithe, and incredibly handsome. Rosencrantz was conducting them as they sang.

'I'm the bestest and wisest man,
Ten times better than Peter Pan,
I've got lots of Frankincense,
I got it on offer for fifty pence,
Is that Jesus in his pram?
He looks like a lump of boiled ham!'

'Mummy, I just taught everyone my brilliant song!' shrilled Rosencrantz when he saw me.

''Ere Coco, I also taught 'im one of mine,' said Ethel. 'Go on, love.'

Rosencrantz didn't need encouragement and he launched straight into it.

'I'm not a pheasant plucker, I'm a pheasant plucker's son,
And I'm only plucking pheasants, till the...'

Rosencrantz tailed off as he noticed the Hamleys bag I was holding.

'Mummy! What's in the bag?' he shrieked, running over and hugging my legs.

'Oh, nothing,' I said holding it up high, out of reach.

'Yer mum's bin shoppin' for Father Christmas,' explained Ethel. I shook my head frantically.

'Oh? What? You 'aven't?' asked Ethel.

It was too much. I burst into tears and ran upstairs. On my way up I heard Ethel say, 'Woss up with 'er? Is it me song? It's not as if I taught 'im the rude version!'

Chris came up and found me a few minutes later. He was carrying a large mug of mulled wine. It smelt delicious.

'Cokes? Hun?' he said, knocking on the bedroom door. He came in, handed me the steaming mug and sat down on the end of the bed. I told him what had happened, ending with running away from the policeman.

'Blimey. Talk about shopping madness...'

'This isn't what Jesus had in mind, is it?' I said.

'Well, technically, Jesus was born in February, wasn't he? And he was Jewish.'

'I don't mean that. Christmas should be a time for caring and sharing. I've left Daniel in an ambulance on Regent Street with a sprained ankle! And what for? A miniature treehouse full of plastic rodents!'

I sat up and showed him the contents of the Hamleys bag.

'What *are* Sylvanian Families?' asked Chris.

'Badgers, and otters, and bears...'

'Oh my,' finished Chris. 'Sounds like a busy night at the Vauxhall tavern.'

'Be serious,' I said, sipping at my mulled wine. 'Ooh that's good, that's *strong*.'

'Why else do you think Ethel is teaching her four-year-old grandson *I'm not a pheasant plucker?* She's on her fourth mug,' said Chris.

I laughed. He went on,

'And Benji has been helping Rosencrantz run through his lines for the Nativity play. He knows them all, and everybody else's... I know we've only been dating for six days, Coco, but I think he's the one. What do you think of him?'

'He's gorgeous, Chris. I'm so pleased for you.'

'He's perfect. And I can't think of a thing I don't like about him. And his body is just amazing. He's so flexible, he can put both legs behind his h—'

The phone began to ring downstairs.

'I'll get it, you lie there and de-compress,' smiled Chris.

He came back a few minutes later.

'Daniel is on his way back in a taxi. He asks if you can come down to the door in ten minutes, with cash. His wallet went missing in the Hamleys melee.'

I sighed and downed my mulled wine.

'I'll get you a refill,' winked Chris.

SUNDAY 20TH DECEMBER

Daniel has a badly sprained ankle. The nurse told him to go home and rest up for a few days. Chris and Benji helped me to get him up the stairs last night and into bed, I then elevated his foot with a pile of old magazines and administered two paracetamol and a glass of brandy, but it didn't seem to help. He was in so much pain. With that, the Tracy Island disaster and the ongoing worry about work next week, I didn't get any sleep beside him.

I'd agreed to go over to Chris's house today and meet Benji properly. Daniel said his foot was giving him agony, and he told me to take Rosencrantz.

'Are you sure you don't want me to stay with you?' I asked.

'No. You go and have fun, Cokes. Mum said she'd pop round. She can look after me properly,' said Daniel.

I was tempted to ask what he meant by *properly?* But I didn't have the energy.

Ethel arrived at two, and only added fuel to the fire by indulging Daniel's groans and mopping his brow. She'd brought an old *Blue Peter* advent crown with balding red tinsel, and proceeded to put it on the bedside table and light the fourth candle.

'Remember this, Danny? You made it when you were little. I thought there should be at least one Christmas decoration in the 'ouse,' said Ethel.

Instead of being Christmassy, it gave the bedroom the air of a nineteenth-century sick bed.

'You go on, Coco. Go 'an 'ave a booze up with Chris. I'm 'ere fer Danny,' said Ethel, pulling up a chair to sit by the bed.

'We're not having a 'booze-up'. I'm only going for an hour, and Rosencrantz wants to go too,' I insisted.

I looked to Rosencrantz for support.

'Yes, I'm coming too, Mummy! I want to see Uncle Chris's tree!' he cried.

I bundled him up against the cold air and we walked round to Chris's through Regent's Park. It was only half two, but the afternoon was beginning to fade and a few ducks were splashing around in the lake.

His house was a blaze of fairy lights when we arrived. The path down to the front door was dotted with dwarves dressed in Santa outfits, the thatch roof was lined with blinking fairy lights, and a wreath on the door said, *'Happy Holidays!'*

When Chris opened the door warm air and the smell of mulled wine rushed out.

'Come in,' he said morosely.

On his hall table was a huge Nativity scene, which on closer inspection I could see was filled with miniature china figurines from Disney's *Beauty and the Beast*. Belle and the Beast were standing by a manger and lying amongst the straw was Chip, the little teacup.

'Isn't baby Jesus supposed to be in the manger?' said Rosencrantz, as I helped him out of his duffle coat.

'And what are the Aristocats doing beside the manger?' I asked.

'My house has been hijacked by Disney,' grimaced Chris. We followed him through to the living room. There was a crackling fire and, beside it, a giant Christmas tree. Disney characters adorned every bauble, and Tinkerbell was on top of the tree waving her magic wand. There were little ornaments of Mickey and Minnie Mouse all along the mantelpiece. On top of the TV was a huge snow globe, and inside was the magic castle from *Sleeping Beauty*.

'Where's Benji?' I asked, as Chris started crashing about in his drinks cabinet.

'I don't know, and I don't care. We had a huge row and he stormed out,' he said, pulling out a huge bottle of Grey Goose vodka.

'Why? Chris, what's going on?' I asked.

'I came back from the gym this morning to find the house like this. Benji had done it for me as a surprise,' he said, slamming down the bottle.

'I think it's quite nice!' cried Rosencrantz, pulling at a bunch of helium balloons floating lazily by the ceiling which had *The Jungle Book* characters on them.

'Yes. I suppose I *should* think it's nice,' said Chris looking around the room with a shudder.

'Are all these decorations his?' I asked, noticing a huge Winnie The Pooh, Tigger and Eeyore sitting on the sofa opposite all dressed in Christmas outfits. Chris pulled out two crystal cut glasses and poured us each a large measure.

'Of course they're all his! All my lovely Conran

decorations are still in the attic... Cokes, it's everywhere. Snow White and the Seven Dwarves in the downstairs loo. A twenty-five-piece Fantasia china dining service in the kitchen. A hundred and one Dalmatians, plus Mr and Mrs Darling and Cruella De Vil on the shelves in the library!' He came over and handed me a vodka, then lowered his voice saying, 'There's even a miniature dolls house in my bedroom which plays 'It's a small world after all' on a loop! What man can maintain an erection with 'It's a small world after all' playing in the background! '

I tried to suppress a laugh.

'It's not funny, Cokes!'

'I know, I'm sorry. Didn't you know Benji was a Disney fan?'

'No! He never mentioned it on our first date.'

'Why would he?'

'Still, look around. Is this normal? He's... He's...'

'A Disney fetishist?' I said.

'Yes!'

We clinked glasses and he took a big gulp of vodka.

'Surely there are worse fetishes, Chris? And you'll sort it out. You're both going on a cruise – you'll only have to look at all this for a day or so. Then you'll be off.'

'I hope so. The alternative is spending Christmas with my family. My sister's just been dumped by a bloke mother disapproved of. I refuse to give her the satisfaction that my relationship is over too,' he said.

'Your relationship with Benji is not over,' I said, adding, 'Who was your sister going out with?'

'Some investment banker. He got bored and left a message on her bleeper that it was over. She booked into The Ritz and tried to kill herself.'

'That's awful! Is she okay?' I asked.

'She's fine. The stupid girl jumped out of a ground-floor window. The only thing she broke was her padded hairband. No, it's going to be okay. I'll just have to learn to cope with Benji's Disney fetish.'

I sat on the sofa and a cushion began to play 'Be Our Guest' from *Beauty and The Beast*.

'Oh!' I cried leaping up.

'Every cushion plays a different tune,' said Chris morosely, throwing it behind the sofa. 'I'll be counting down the hours until we're cruising through the Caribbean islands.'

'I can't wait to open my Tracy Island!' piped up Rosencrantz as he twiddled the baubles on the tree.

'Shit!' I mouthed to Chris.

'Oh, that reminds me. Dad's been in touch,' said Chris in a low voice.

'Yes?' I said eagerly.

'Not good news: your island is like gold dust apparently. They've been changing hands on the black market for hundreds of pounds. He's going to keep an eye out, but don't hold your breath.'

We stayed for a couple of hours, then Benji returned and it was all a bit frosty so I said we'd head back home.

'Will I see you at Christmas, Uncle Christopher?' asked Rosencrantz.

'I'll see you tomorrow,' said Chris. 'I'm coming to watch you in your Nativity play.'

Rosencrantz beamed. 'Yay!'

'And I'm coming too,' said Benji pointedly, looking at Chris.

'It will be lovely to see you both,' I said.

'Although please don't be disappointed,' said Rosencrantz seriously. 'Mary and Joseph have no chemistry...'

Chris and Benji looked at me and we all laughed.

'What? It's true!' insisted Rosencrantz. 'I overheard Miss Mears talking to the Headmistress.'

As we walked back home in the dark, Rosencrantz asked what it meant for Mary and Joseph to have no chemistry. Before I could stop myself I said that they didn't have a chemist's shop near them in Bethlehem. Then we saw two very posh ladies whose little dogs had decided to have rampant sex by the pond.

'What are those doggies doing, Mummy?' asked Rosencrantz.

'They're doing the conga,' I said.

'That's a bit different to how we did it at my birthday party...'

'Yes, dogs, um, do it differently because they don't usually have any music,' I said.

He seemed satisfied and we carried on past the two posh ladies who had given up trying to separate their dogs. It made me think, why do we lie to kids all the time? That was the third lie I'd told Rosencrantz today. Did it really protect him, lying? Although the Tracy Island lie was justified because I was determined to get him one for Christmas. As far as the dogs were concerned, I didn't want to have to go into the birds and the bees, not yet. And as for Mary and Joseph, well, life was too short to worry about two little kids who can't act.

And who'd want their child to go into the acting profession anyway?

When we got home, Ethel met us at the door. The house was in darkness. I flicked the light switch but nothing happened.

'Has there been a power cut?' I asked.

She looked terrified and grabbed me, whispering, 'Yes! And iss Danny! I think 'e's possessed, Coco!'

She was wearing her plastic rain hood indoors and clutching her little crucifix.

'What?' I said.

''E's been babbling nonsense for the past hour, well, not the usual shite, *real* nonsense...'

Candles were dotted about, casting a dim glow, and we followed her upstairs and into the bedroom. Daniel was lying in bed. His skin had a horrible grey hue and he was soaked in sweat.

'Oola baloolaer ranticfah!' he murmured. 'Wooohoo pallooo!'

''E's talkin' Latin, Coco,' said Ethel. ''E must be possessed, cos 'e failed the eleven plus. 'E never did Latin... only woodwork.'

'He sounds delirious,' I said.

Ethel went to the end of the bed and lifted the covers.

'No! Look. A face 'as appeared on the bed sheets! It's Jesus!' she hissed with wonder in her eyes.

I joined her and together we peered at the spot she was indicating on the sheet. There was a black stain, an eerie, angular pleading face with long hair. Beside it Daniel's foot was propped up on the pile of magazines, looking puce and hugely swollen.

'Cantoono baramshifah!' gurgled Daniel menacingly. 'Rambabba-booba!' The candles flickered on the *Blue Peter* advent crown.

'Mummy, I'm a bit scared,' said Rosencrantz grabbing at my leg.

The candles flickered again and Daniel groaned. Suddenly

all the lights came back on. I peered closer at the face on the bed sheet again.

'That's not Jesus, it's Yoko Ono,' I said.

'Eh?' said Ethel.

'Did you move the pile of magazines?'

'Yeah. Danny was 'avin cramp,' she said.

I gently pulled out a magazine from the bottom of the pile.

'Look. It's the ink from the *Radio Times*,' I said. 'It's transferred onto the bed sheet.'

Sure enough, it was an article and a picture of Yoko Ono. Ethel seemed to blame me that her son wasn't possessed, and got very huffy.

'Can you blame me fer worrying?'

I went to him and felt his head. He was burning up.

'He's definitely delirious,' I said. 'I think we should ring the doctor.'

The doctor came, reluctantly, but when he saw Daniel and the state of his foot, he called for an ambulance. We followed to the hospital and waited for several hours in the busy waiting room. Ethel kept repeating, 'I told yer it was bad. Didn't I?'

'Okay, let's just wait and keep calm,' I said, glad that Rosencrantz was out of earshot. He was blissfully unaware and playing on an activity centre in the corner of the waiting room.

When a doctor finally came out, he told us that Daniel had broken his ankle and had an infection.

''E's not gonna die?' asked Ethel.

'No. We've set the bone and given him a cast. He's also on intravenous antibiotics,' said the doctor. 'We'll be keeping him in overnight for observation.'

'Thank you, Doctor, praise the Lord. 'Is wife 'ere, she

didn't think it was anything serious, but I... all I can say is that I probably saved 'is life!' exclaimed Ethel.

I bit my tongue.

'Can we see him, Doctor,' I asked through gritted teeth.

'Of course, but he's very tired,' said the doctor.

He took us through to the ward where Daniel lay looking a little better. But his leg! He had a plaster cast from his knee down to his foot! It was hung from a loop attached to the ceiling. I felt a sudden rush of love for him. There was a brief tussle between me and Ethel, but I made it to his bedside first so she had to scuttle round to the other side.

'Hello love,' I said, smoothing his dark hair down. 'I thought you were being over-dramatic... I love you.'

'It's okay, Cokes. It's going to be an interesting Christmas, eh?' he said, smiling weakly.

'We'll all be there for yer, Danny. Meryl an' Tony are comin' down, and little Rosencrantz is 'ere,' she said, leaning in front of me and stroking his hair.

'I'll be there too,' I said.

'Blood is thicker than water though, Danny,' said Ethel.

And no one is thicker than you, Ethel, I wanted to say, but I bit my lip.

We stayed with him for a while, competing for who had the best bedside manner. Then Daniel asked Ethel if she would take Rosencrantz home and put him to bed. Ethel was a bit put out at this, but capitulated, and after Rosencrantz gave Daniel a big hug, they left.

'Go easy on Mum. She had a fright,' said Daniel.

'I had a fright too,' I said. 'You know, I've tried until I'm blue in the face with your mother...'

'She's old, Coco.'

ROBERT BRYNDZA

'She's not really that old, Daniel.'

'Yeah, but she's lonely. Dad's been dead a long time. Meryl lives up in Milton Keynes. I think she feels I'm all she's got.'

'Well, just remember you've got me and Rosencrantz too. Everything seems to be getting out of control. The most important thing is our health and our happiness. Look, I know this is difficult, but can we talk about your mum...'

There was a soft sound of snoring, and Daniel was asleep.

'Every time I try to talk to you about Ethel, you fall asleep,' I said.

I stayed with him for a little longer, then I kissed the top of his sleeping head and left.

When I came out of the hospital, a Salvation Army band was huddled under the awning playing 'Silent Night'. The sound of the brass instruments was so rich and warm, compared to the cold evening. I lit up a cigarette and stopped and listened for a while. It was the song Dad always put on the record player as we decorated the tree. I was overcome with sadness, and anger. Sadness that my parents weren't here to see Rosencrantz grow up, and anger that they'd left me.

When I arrived home, the house was quiet. I went upstairs, and Ethel was coming out of Rosencrantz's bedroom. She was holding a copy of *The Very Hungry Caterpillar* in one hand and an ashtray with three cigarette butts in the other.

'What are you doing?' I asked.

'I just read Rosencrantz a story; 'e was out like a light,' said Ethel.

'No, what are you doing with that ashtray? Were you smoking in his bedroom?'

'No, I weren't smoking in 'is bedroom!' she hissed.

I followed her down the stairs.

'Then why are you carrying the ashtray?'

'Iss my ashtray! I was tidying up. Something you'd know all about if you was even a little 'ouse proud! When did you last push the carpet sweeper round?'

'No! You do NOT get to speak to me like that in my house!' I hissed back.

'Oh gawd Coco, take it out on me!'

'Take it out on you? That's my son!'

'An' my grandson! An' I would NEVER smoke in 'is room!' she said.

'Oh really? I know for a fact you smoked like a chimney when Daniel and Meryl were babies. Daniel told me you used to balance an ashtray on his head when you breastfed him.'

'You watch yer mouth, Coco! We didn't know 'ow bad smoking was back then!'

'In all his baby pictures the top of his head is completely flat!'

'That was the forceps!' she snarled. We glared at each other, then she went on, 'If I'm such a bad mother, why was I the only one with Danny? I knew 'e was in a bad way! I knew it were more than a sprain. You were off gallivanting with that Chris!'

'You also thought he was possessed by the devil! Or Yoko Ono. You're obviously too bloody thick to tell the difference!'

We had reached the front door now. Ethel grabbed her coat off the peg and dragged the door open.

'Where are you going? It's eleven o'clock at night?' I said.

'Well, I'm not stayin' ere! To think of all I've done for you!'

'What have you done for me? You're always here, criticising and making snide comments!'

'I'm good enough whenever you want a babysitter though, ain't I? You know I've got a life too!'

She stomped off to the gate.

'Ethel, please, it's late... Stay and let's talk, sensibly.'

'I know when I'm not welcome! You think I'm muck, don't yer?'

'I do not think that!' I shouted.

A taxi was rounding the corner; she flagged it down and got in. I watched it drive away into the cold night. I came back in and closed the door.

I went upstairs to Rosencrantz's room. His small form shifted under the blanket. There was a faint smell of cigarettes, but I couldn't tell if it was coming off me. I opened his window a little and let some air in. The moon was high in the sky and frost glittered on the rooftops stretching out across London. I put my head against the window frame and drank in the silence. Very softly the opening strains of 'Silent Night' floated on the breeze from next door. When it got to 'All is calm, all is bright', there was the sound of a needle being yanked off a record. Then I heard Mrs Cohen shout, 'Stop playing that rubbish and help me find the candles for the Menorah!'

A row started up so I closed the window. I went to Rosencrantz's bedside and looked at him sleeping peacefully, his beautiful little face lit up by the moonlight.

'Do you know how much you are loved?' I said softly. 'I would die for you. So would your Dad, and, I hate to say it, your Nan too... I wish that meant something to you right now. But you're lucky to be young enough not to know heartbreak, or loss, or pain. I'm doing everything I can to get you Tracy Island. I just hope that it doesn't break your little heart if I can't.'

I kissed Rosencrantz and came downstairs. Apart from Ethel's *Blue Peter* advent crown, you wouldn't know it was Christmas in the house. I came into the kitchen and made myself a cup of cocoa. I slumped into a chair and pulled out a pad and a pencil to see what needed to be done before Christmas:

1. Find Tracy Island urgently!!!!
2. As an absolute last resort, find Blue Peter plans to *make* Tracy Island.
3. Make Rosencrantz's Nativity play outfit, wash bed sheet and tea towel, also hunt down gold curtain tie-back which will make a good belt. (Is the school supplying the wise men's gifts? If not who sells Frankincense? Debenhams?)
4. Buy a nice real Christmas tree of aesthetically pleasing proportions and decorate. Decorate house.
5. Buy all Christmas food/booze and other presents.
6. Check fold-up Z beds for when the in-laws come to stay, and throw away faulty one. If Daniel's sister Meryl gets trapped in folding contraption like last year, I will never hear the end of it.
7. Visit local library and look for self-help books about coping with an awful mother-in-law. Also hide the Christmas *Radio Times* before Ethel gets to it with her highlighter pen.
8. Buy blank videotapes, which can be used as a bargaining tool if we have a clash of Christmas TV programmes. Work out how to use video recorder.
9. Buy crackers.
10. Try not to go crackers.
11. Replacement bulbs for fairy lights.
12. Buy Pic N Mix from Woolworths for carol singers.
13. Find nice Christmas music cassette.

14. Present for Rosencrantz's teacher?
15. Who is Rosencrantz's teacher? Ugh. Am a terrible mother.

Then the pencil broke. I put my head on the table and burst into tears.

MONDAY 21ST DECEMBER

I woke up this morning with my head on the table, fully-dressed. I had been dreaming I was on a beach. I could feel the sun warm on my face, but now I could feel my face was stuck to something. I opened my eyes and saw it was the Argos Christmas catalogue.

'Mummy, shouldn't I be at school?' I heard a voice say.

I turned to see Rosencrantz in the kitchen doorway. He had got himself up and dressed, and it was eight o'clock. Everything came flooding back to me: Daniel was in hospital... the row with Ethel... Rosencrantz had to be at school... I had to be at school... Tracy Island... Christmas still had to be assembled.

'Shit!' I said. 'Shit, shit, shit, shit, shit!'

'Mummy, you shouldn't use those words,' he said.

'Yes, they're only for mummies to use,' I agreed.

I grabbed my purse and my keys and drove him round to school. Luckily, I looked like all the other mothers on the school run – harassed and bedraggled, and several of them were still wearing slippers. I came back home to grab the rest of my stuff when the phone rang. It was Meryl.

'Helllloooo Coco!' she trilled. I could hear Nat King Cole in the background singing 'It's Beginning to Look a Lot Like Christmas'.

'Meryl, I can't stop. I'm on my way out to work,' I said.

'This is just a quickie, Coco. I won't keep you. I wanted to ask if you have a memory foam pillow?'

'I thought you said you were getting me and Daniel bath cubes for Christmas?'

'Yes! Of course we are. No, this is a memory foam pillow for Tony, he's suffering terrible whiplash.'

'Did he have an accident in the hearse?'

'No, he went a bit overboard doing the funky chicken at the Rotary Club Christmas dinner and dance... If you ask me he was playing to the crowd, but the only people he comes into contact with at work are dead, so I let him have his moment in the sun.'

'Meryl, I'm late for work—' I said.

'Okay working girl, can you put Daniel on?'

I quickly told her everything that had happened.

'Oh Coco, that's awful,' she said. 'Well, look, I can help ease the burden...' I thought she was going to say that she and Tony wouldn't be coming to stay for ten days, but instead she offered to talk to Mandy at Handy Mandy Crafts, her local craft shop.

'I could help you make Tracy Island!' she added excitedly. 'Now I've mastered Batik and finger puppets, I'm dying for a challenge—'

'Meryl I've got to go,' I said.

'Righty-ho. Well, keep me in the loop about Daniel, I'll

bring that pillow for Tony, and start to brainstorm Tracy Island... byeeeee!'

I got to work at nine o'clock. Marika, God bless her, had somehow managed to take the register for my class and get them seated for assembly in an orderly fashion. She'd saved me a chair beside her at the side of the hall.

'Thank you,' I whispered as we took our seats and The Ripper appeared at the front. She smiled and handed me a tissue.

'You've got 'sogra' written on your forehead,' she murmured.

I grabbed the tissue and scrubbed at it.

'All gone?' I whispered. She nodded. 'I fell asleep on the Argos catalogue,' I added.

I didn't get to hear her response because we all stood for the first hymn, 'God Rest Ye Merry Gentlemen'.

The rest of the day was a crazy blur. All the teachers bunged on videos for their classes to watch and we took it in turns to keep an eye on the kids whilst we tried to organise our lives. I nipped out to Debenhams and bought a pillowcase and tea towel for Rosencrantz's Wise Man outfit. I checked the toy department, but was laughed at when I asked if they had any Tracy Islands.

I bumped into Mr Wednesday, the handsome art teacher, on one of his rare visits to the staffroom and he kindly said he would photocopy me the *Blue Peter* 'make your own' Tracy Island plans. He's very rugged and tanned with a shock of dark hair. He smells delicious and carries a leather satchel with a selection of Koh-i-Noor pencils poking out, and I sometimes see him sharpening one with a Swiss army knife.

'Come and see me in the art room,' he grinned, his white teeth contrasting with his black stubble.

'Yes, I will,' I said, feeling rather overwhelmed by him.

At lunchtime I phoned the hospital who told me that Daniel was doing well and could probably be discharged tomorrow. I said to tell him I would visit after work. Marika had asked if I had a moment before I left, but I completely forgot and dashed off as soon as the bell went for the end of the day.

I picked up Rosencrantz from school and took him straight over to see Daniel. He was sitting up in his hospital bed and looked almost back to normal.

'Daddy!' Rosencrantz yelled and went to jump on the bed.

'No!' said Daniel, and I grabbed him quickly before he could land on his cast.

On the bedside table, I noticed there was a huge bowl of fruit, a giant 'get well' card and several bottles of Lucozade.

'Mum's been here most of the day,' said Daniel. 'Got me a lovely card too.'

I realised I hadn't brought him anything. I also realised the time.

'I'm sorry, Daniel, it's been a mad day, and we can only stay for a few minutes...'

'I'm due on stage tonight,' said Rosencrantz proudly.

'Yes. Break a leg son,' said Daniel. 'I wish I could come and see you!'

'Don't break a leg, Rosencrantz. I couldn't cope with you both in plaster,' I said.

'Mummy, *break a leg* is just a figure of speech. It means good luck before a performance.'

Daniel and I laughed.

'Bye Daddy!' he yelled and gave Daniel a kiss.

'See you tomorrow, love you,' I said, pecking him on the cheek.

'Yes, Cokes, love you too,' he said.

When we got home, I assembled Rosencrantz's Wise Man outfit and got ready for the Nativity. He looked so adorable! I got changed and then we drove over to the school. Chris and Benji were waiting for us outside and when Rosencrantz saw them he suddenly got very scared and tearful.

'Mummy, what if I forget what I have to say!' he said, the panic on his face.

'You won't forget,' I said. 'You know your lines better than anyone. And you know all theirs too!'

'Yes, Rosencrantz. Just take a deep breath and enjoy it,' said Chris.

'But what if I do forget?' asked Rosencrantz, wiping away the tears in his little eyes with the corner of his Wise Man's tea-towel headdress.

'Then improvise,' said Benji.

'What does that mean?' asked Rosencrantz.

'You know the story so you can make up something that fits,' said Benji.

'You'll be fine, you're the best little actor I know,' said Chris, giving him a hug.

I took Rosencrantz round to the classroom and reluctantly left him with Miss Mears. Then we took our seats in the school hall front of the stage. It looked magical. Fairy lights and paper lanterns hung from the ceiling, and the scenery on stage was an image of the mountains of Bethlehem, with a star in the sky. When Benji went off to get us all a cup of mulled wine, I asked Chris if things were okay between them.

'Yes, we made up when he came home, three times. I can think of worse things to be obsessed with than Disney... He could have wanted me to pee on him!'

A rather posh lady next to us choked into our mulled wine. Chris didn't seem to notice and carried on,

'How are things with you? By the way, where is Ethel?'

'Good point,' I said. 'I thought she'd be here...'

'Here, use my mobile phone?' offered Chris, retrieving it from his long coat and pulling up the aerial.

I dialled Ethel's number and she answered after a few rings.

'Oo is it?'

'Ethel, it's me. I'm at Rosencrantz's Nativity play. Where are you?'

'Well, as far as I remember, I'm not welcome!' she snapped and hung up. I stared at the phone in shock.

'She's not coming,' I said to Chris. 'She can hate me all she wants, but Rosencrantz wants her to be here.'

Then Benji appeared with the mulled wine and the lights dimmed so I didn't get to say anymore.

There was a pause. Then the music began, and a spotlight came on up on a rotund little redheaded girl wearing a pillowcase and tinfoil angel wings, who began to narrate the play.

The children were all very sweet, but I think Miss Mears took it all a bit too seriously with the live Dulux dogs around the manger, and we had no idea that Mary was going to give birth to a real live baby.

'Ouch. And she did it without gas and air,' whispered Chris when the tiny girl playing Mary was presented with a very large thirteen-month-old toddler, who apparently belonged to one of the school dinner ladies.

We all gave a squeal when the Wise Men arrived.

'Rosencrantz looks the best, like a tiny Arab,' said Chris.

'Is he wearing a curtain tie-back from Debenhams? I love their living room range,' added Benji.

'Yes,' I said, welling up with pride.

And then Rosencrantz started speaking!!!

'On this special night, under a banker of stars,' he began. He took a breath... Then there was silence. Rosencrantz froze. There was a shuffling of feet and several people in the audience coughed.

'Did he mean to say 'bank' of stars or 'blanket'?' I whispered.

'It should be blanket,' whispered Benji.

'Ummm,' quavered Rosencrantz, biting his lip. The silence went on.

'Where's the bloody prompt?' I hissed.

Chris grabbed my hand. Rosencrantz looked around at the silence. His bottom lip trembled. Tears came into his eyes.

'You know your lines,' I whispered loudly, smiling and trying to catch his eye to reassure him.

'Improvise!' whispered Benji, equally loudly.

Rosencrantz tried to see past the bright lights to where we sat.

'Yes, improvise Rosencrantz!' hissed Chris.

'Sing your little song,' I said, more loudly.

Rosencrantz gulped and seemed to compose himself. He took a deep breath and said,

I'm not a pleasant fucker, I'm a pleasant fucker's son,

And I'm only fucking pleasant 'til the pleasant fucker comes!' he beamed and handed the Frankincense to Mary.

The next little Wise Man stepped forward grinning and started, 'I'm not a pleasant fucker, I'm—'

The curtains suddenly began to whirr shut, sweeping together at speed and, in their haste, dragging over the microphones on stands at the front of the stage. There was a crashing, echoing sound and then feedback. The headmistress leapt up from her seat, and told everyone how wonderful it had been and refreshments would be served outside the hall.

Myself, Chris and Benji helped ourselves to another plastic cup of mulled wine and waited for Rosencrantz to emerge. We were given a wide berth by everyone in the hall. No one said a thing. As if what Rosencrantz had said was supposed to be in the script, and people were politely ignoring this radical bit in the story. Rosencrantz came out, still in his costume, and ran to me and cuddled my legs.

'I'm sorry Mummy, I think I got the Pheasant Plucker rhyme wrong?'

'Yes, but never mind. Maybe you should have sung your made-up song, *I'm the best and wisest man, ten times better than Peter Pan,'* I said.

'It was the only thing I could remember,' he said, sadly. 'Did I let you down, Mummy?'

'Of course not!' I said, crouching down to hug him.

'It was scary up there, Mummy...'

I noticed we were getting haughty looks from the Headmistress. I got up to go and say something to her, but Chris grabbed my arm.

'Come on Cokes, let's go. Your mouth will only make things worse.'

Outside on the street we said goodbye to Chris and Benji.

'We'll try and phone you from the cruise ship,' said Chris.

Several parents walked past us and stared at Rosencrantz, the little foul-mouthed Wise Man. An elderly bloke with a kind face stopped and told us how much more interesting the Nativity had been this year, then walked off into the dark with his wife.

'What did I do?' asked Rosencrantz in wonder.

'You went down in Nativity play history Rosencrantz,' said Benji. 'I'd kill for an audience to go away remembering me like that!'

Rosencrantz tilted his head up to me, peering from under his bobble hat.

'I don't understand, Mummy? I thought I made a mistake,' he said.

'I'll tell you when you're older,' I said, squatting down to give him a kiss. Chris squatted down too.

'Have a fabulous Christmas, Rosencrantz,' he said. 'What do you think of Scalextric? I've heard they are *really* cool...'

'What's a Scaleytrix?' he said.

'Oh, well it's... um, something to do with travel?'

'Electric car racing,' I said, saving Chris.

'Yeah! And I hear that Father Christmas has plenty in stock!' he added.

'No. I want Tracy Island and I've written to Father Christmas weeks ago. As Nan says, if you want something you have to book it well in advance. Where is Nan?'

'She, um, wasn't feeling well,' I said.

'Shame, cos I really, really wanted her here. Just as much as I really, really want Tracy Island,' he said. 'FIVE.... FOUR.... THREE...TWO... ONE. THUNDERBIRDS ARE GO!'

He went tearing off round the school car park, his gold curtain tie-back belt dragging along behind him. Benji and Chris looked at me sympathetically.

'I'm going to have to make it,' I said. 'I've got the Art teacher, Tom Wednesday, to give me the plans.'

'Yes, *Tom Wednesday*,' said Chris. 'Bit of a dish, Benji.'

'Ooh. What does he look like?' asked Benji.

'He's dark and quiet. Tall. Rolls his shirt sleeves up and has lovely arms. He's very much like, the kind of man who you see in *The National Geographic* magazine, advertising precision watches, or steering a ship,' I said.

'Ooh, an intrepid explorer,' said Benji.

'Yes, do you think he wants to explore you? Intrepidly, Cokes?' joked Chris.

'I'm married,' I said. 'And he's... he's... Mr Wednesday.'

'He could be Mister Any-day-of-the-week for some lucky lady,' said Chris. 'He owns his own yacht, Benji!'

'Oh! You could be Tom Wednesday's Girl Friday!' cried Benji.

'I doubt it. Right now I feel more like Gayle Tuesday...' I said.

I bade them farewell and Rosencrantz and I headed home.

When we arrived at the front door, an ambulance was parked by the kerb and a paramedic was helping Daniel out.

'Daddy!' shouted Rosencrantz.

Daniel grimaced in pain as he stepped down onto the pavement. He had a paper bag containing his things under his arm.

'I'll leave him with you then,' said the paramedic. He got into the ambulance and drove off.

'Didn't they give you a crutch?' I asked, as Daniel stood there in his pyjamas resting his huge cast on the kerb.

'Oh bugger, it was in the ambulance,' he said. 'Where's Mum?'

'She didn't show up,' I said.

'That's odd. She said she was going. Didn't you offer to give her a lift?'

'No. She gets the bus everywhere.'

'It's late, Coco. So she missed the Nativity?'

'Yes.'

There was a silence. He grabbed my arm and we made it slowly up the steps to the front door, his leg with the cast lurching, and our little Wise Man following with the paper bag.

When we got in, I told Rosencrantz to get ready for bed. Daniel slumped on the sofa and we had a huge row. He thought it was my fault Ethel didn't feel she could come to Rosencrantz's school Nativity! Halfway through the row Daniel began to grimace.

'What is it? Do you want painkillers?' I asked.

'I've got a crazy itch,' he groaned, rubbing at the plaster cast.

'Do you want me to get you a knitting needle?' I asked. Then I realised I never knitted. I went through to the kitchen and grabbed a few bits of cutlery, a pencil, a ruler and the barbecue tongs. When I got back in the living room, Rosencrantz had changed into his pyjamas and was trying to help.

'What about a ruler?' suggested Rosencrantz.

'Try this,' I said, handing a rather short ruler to Daniel.

It wasn't big enough, nor were the cutlery items. We spent an hour trying to find something to scratch Daniel's itch, but nothing was long enough. Not even the barbecue tongs, which, with difficulty, I bent out to their full length. Then Rosencrantz went to bed and the row restarted about Ethel. He refuses to believe the woman is capable of doing wrong.

Daniel ended up sleeping downstairs on one of the Z-beds.

I came upstairs, checked on Rosencrantz, and then got in bed alone.

Just before I went to sleep I remembered Mr Wednesday had something very long: the rod he uses to open the skylight in his classroom. It would fit perfectly down the side of Daniel's plaster cast.

TUESDAY 22ND DECEMBER

I was late again, and Marika covered for me, again. I did have two very good reasons: an invalid husband who needed help to wash and dress, and a four-year-old son who'd said the F-word four times during a primary school Nativity play.

When I dropped Rosencrantz off, I went into school to assure the Headmistress that it was a silly mistake, that Rosencrantz didn't even know what he was saying, and that it wasn't the beginning of a darker pattern of behaviour.

Thank God it was the last day of term! There was such a nice atmosphere at school. The death knell of a redundancy had failed to chime, so I was now certain The Ripper had just been scaring me into handing over Tracy Island. In the morning after registration, the kids all went to the assembly hall, again, to watch films. The teachers took it in turns to nip out for a last-minute errand, a fag and a coffee, but in my case I went to find Mr Wednesday to get the plans for Tracy Island. I'd been told he was in the art room firing the jugs, fruit bowls and ashtrays made by pupils.

The art room was tucked away at the back of the school

buildings. When I walked in, the lights were off. I moved past dimly-lit easels set up around a now-dismantled still life of driftwood and leaves. I could just make out paintings and drawings lining the walls, and there was a sink in the corner, completely filthy from endless dirty paintbrushes. At the back was a glass partition and, behind it, almost in darkness, the giant grey dome of the kiln hummed.

As I got closer I could feel the heat rolling across the room. I jumped when the door of the kiln opened, and a bright square of orange lit up the art room. Mr Wednesday stood there, stripped down to his waist, and bathed in the glow. Sweat shone on his quite remarkable torso. *How does he get so muscly doing fine pencil drawings?* I thought. He noticed me and closed the kiln, bathing us in darkness.

'Hello, Mrs Pinchard,' he said, coming round the glass partition and wiping sweat off his face with a muscly forearm. 'Sorry,' he added, indicating his lack of shirt. 'It gets so bloody boiling when the kiln is on.'

'Oh, it's okay,' I said.

I was glad it was quite dark, so he couldn't see that I was blushing. He went over to his desk and started to rifle through piles of paperwork. He flicked on a lamp. I went and joined him. His battered leather satchel was on the side, and next to it was a picture of him grinning beside a large sailing boat. He was wearing shorts and a white woolly jumper, his thick, dark hair being blown to one side by the wind.

'Is this your boat?' I asked.

'Yes. *Odessa*. She's my saviour from work. I'm hoping I can take her out over Christmas, if it's not too choppy.'

'She's beautiful. I'd love to go down on her...' I froze when I realised what I'd said. 'I mean, of course, to go down into her *bows*, you know, inside her, it, the boat—'

'It's okay, I know what you meant,' he laughed, still searching around on his desk, 'Ah. Here we go.'

He picked up the photocopy of the plans for Tracy Island.

'How many pages is it?' I said, dismayed.

'Eleven. But if you go through slowly you'll be fine. There's a list of all the materials you need at the back.'

He flicked through the plans, but they slipped from his hand and fell to the floor, sliding in all directions across the waxed parquet floor. We both went off in different directions to retrieve the pages.

'Here, I'll staple them,' he said, moving back to his desk and putting them in order. I spied a sheet we'd missed under the desk, and ducked down to retrieve it.

The fluorescent lights suddenly came on, flicking separately until they lit the room in unison.

'Mr Wednesday,' said a female voice, 'why did you have the lights off?'

I crawled out from under the desk, emerging at the flies of Mr Wednesday's trousers. He was still naked from the waist up. Miss Bruce took one look at us, cried 'Disgusting!' and left. Her clumpy court shoes thudding rapidly away to silence.

'I'm so sorry,' said Mr Wednesday, 'that must have looked really suspect.'

'Yes, don't you worry, you'll be the hero. I'll be the one who's known for doing goodness knows what to the Art teacher under his desk.'

'And you were just talking about going down,' he joked.

I stood up and our eyes met. I suddenly wished I could step out of my life. Spend a week with this handsome, thrilling man on his boat. Very slowly he leaned in to kiss me.

'I'm married, I'm sorry,' I said, pulling back and shaking the thought away.

'I know. It's a shame, because you're really beautiful,' he said softly.

I looked up into his eyes, which were a remarkable shade of blue. His bare chest was still damp with sweat.

'Thank you,' I said.

'What for?'

'For making me feel like a person. Not a crap teacher or a crap mother or a crap daughter-in-law and wife.'

'No one needs to know,' he said softly, leaning in to kiss me again.

'Sorry. No,' I said.

I took a deep breath, turned and walked quickly away, closing the door to the art room behind me.

I went straight to the ladies loos and splashed cold water on my face. My heart was pounding. *Did that just happen?* I thought. As I pulled out one of those horrible rough paper towels to dry my face, a toilet flushed and Marika emerged from a cubicle.

'Hello. You all right?' I said.

She looked like death. Pale with huge bags under her eyes.

'Electricity still isn't back on,' she said. 'I haven't slept.'

'Or eaten, by the look of it.'

She turned on the warm water and put her hands under. Steam rose up and misted the base of the mirror; she kept her hands there, seemingly to thaw out.

'I've been meaning to say thanks, for all the help with covering my absences,' I said. She smiled, still warming her hands under the water. 'And, what are you doing for Christmas?' I asked.

'My Christmas or your Christmas?'

'How do you mean?'

'We celebrate it on the twenty-fourth in Slovakia,' she said.

'Oh, I didn't know. So what are you doing?'

'I'll be at home,' she said, without a trace of wanting pity.

'Do you want to come to mine after work? You can have a shower. I was going to get fish and chips... '

'No, you've got so much to do and you've got a family,' she said.

'You could sleep on the sofa. Oh, actually Daniel's downstairs on the Z-bed...'

'I can get the last tube home from yours,' she smiled. 'Thank you,'

'So that means you'll come, after school?'

'Yes,' she grinned.

The rest of the day went by like a flash. Miss Bruce was nowhere to be seen in the staffroom at lunchtime. The school nurse had sent her home after having 'a funny turn'. When I'd done afternoon registration, each of my kids presented me with chocolate. I had thirty boxes. I was incredibly touched. Damian Grange had managed to get a very good pirate copy of *Terminator 2*, so I put it on the video player in my form room and I opened some of my chocolates to share with the kids.

'You know, you're actually quite cool, Miss,' said Kelly Roffey. Coming from Kelly Roffey, it was quite a compliment.

When the bell rang at three-thirty I waved goodbye to the kids, and went through to the staffroom, where plastic cups of lukewarm wine were being passed out by Mrs Carter.

'Cheers, and thank God it's the end of term,' she said downing hers in one, adding, 'Right, I'm off. I've got Five Tracy Islands to make!'

'And here's to Miss Bruce!' added Mr Gutteridge raising his cup.

'Why are you toasting her?' asked Marika, joining our group and taking a cup of wine.

'She's gone and taken early retirement after all,' explained Mr Gutteridge. 'I saw her on the way to the Art department earlier, and she seemed fine... Then, all of a sudden, she's been in to see the Headmaster and tells him she's going. She took a train to Whitstable.'

'What's in Whitstable?' I asked.

'Not Tom Wednesday; I think she rather held a candle for him. God knows what happened in the Art room,' said Mrs Carter winding up her scarf and pulling on a pair of warm gloves.

'But she's old,' said Marika.

'You'll be old one day too,' mused Mr Gutteridge, swilling the dregs of his wine round then knocking them back. 'Creeps up on all of us.'

'So no one's being made redundant?' I asked.

'No. Merry Christmas,' said Mr Gutteridge, mournfully slopping more wine into his cup.

We finished our wine, wished everyone a happy Christmas, and then I drove Marika back to the house.

'You live *here?*' said Marika as we pulled into Steeplejack Mews. She craned her neck at the size of the houses.

'It was Mum and Dad's house,' I said. 'I got it when they passed away. Did I tell you that Daniel has been in hospital?'

We pulled up near the front door, and parked outside was a hearse.

'Oh my God,' I gasped.

'What? He's dead?' cried Marika, going all wide-eyed.

'What? No! It's my in-laws...'

'They're dead?' said Marika.

'No. They're here.'

'I still don't understand,' shrugged Marika.

I explained that Meryl and Tony run a funeral parlour in

94

Milton Keynes and that they are too tight to buy another car so they go everywhere in the hearse.

'They always get into rows with the management at Sainsbury's when they take up two parking spaces,' I said.

'Maybe I should go home,' said Marika, nervously.

'No. You are my friend. They're the ones who've arrived a day early,' I said.

When we opened the front door I nearly bashed Daniel's leg. He was sitting at the bottom of the stairs with his cast sticking out in front. Tony was sitting two stairs up playing snap with Rosencrantz. All the other doors leading off the hallway were closed.

'Snap, Uncle Tony!' cried Rosencrantz.

'Bloody hell,' said Tony. 'Ah Coco.' He squeezed down the stairs, past Daniel to give me a lingering hug. His red face leered over Marika. 'And who is this lovely young lady?'

'Marika Rolincova,' said Marika, offering her hand.

Tony bent down and kissed it. He stood back up but kept hold of her hand.

'Do I detect an accent?' he said.

'Yes, Slovak.'

'Ah, Czechoslovakia,' said Tony, getting all bug-eyed and excited. 'Our knives and forks all have 'Made in Czechoslovakia' written on them. Is it written somewhere on you?'

'What?' said Marika.

The living room door flew open and Meryl stood there in her housecoat winding up the hoover cord.

'Tony! What are you doing?'

Tony leapt away from Marika, and I introduced her to Meryl.

'Oh, you're a foreigner, how interesting. Nice to meet

you... Don't flush the downstairs loo, I've only just put Harpic down. Don't go in the kitchen, the floor's wet, and you'd better steer clear of the lounge too, I've just shampooed the carpet. It was a bit of a fright, Coco.'

Marika looked confused as Meryl leant in and kissed us both.

'You were bloody quick, Auntie Meryl,' said Rosencrantz.

'No toilet language, *please* Rosencrantz,' she said.

'That's nothing, Auntie Meryl, apparently I said loads of rude words in the school Nativity play!'

'He's joking,' I said, putting my hand over his little mouth.

Meryl pushed past Daniel with the hoover.

'Right, I'll get cracking on your pelmets, Coco. Tony, you can make yourself useful and find the crevice tool!'

He leapt to attention and followed Meryl up the stairs.

I looked at Daniel.

'What are they doing here?' I hissed. He shifted, trying to get comfortable with his leg poking out. 'Couldn't you have pretended to be out?'

'She heard me watching *Countdown*,' he said.

'Who fancies a swift one on the corner?' I suggested. 'If she's going to clean, we might as well let her get on with it.'

'Yeah, I'm spitting feathers,' said Daniel, rising awkwardly.

'What? What's a swift one on the corner? And why would it have feathers? asked Marika anxiously.

'Mummy means do you want to have a booze drink at the pub on the corner, and Daddy said he's thirsty. I'm coming too, but I'm only going to have a children's drink,' said Rosencrantz, taking Marika's hand. 'Come on, I'll look after you,' he added. Marika grinned.

Even though the pub was close, it took a while to help Daniel hobble the short way there. I ordered wine for Marika and me, a pint for Daniel, and Vimto and crisps for Rosencrantz. We sat at a cosy table in the corner.

'I know that bloody is toilet language,' announced Rosencrantz, fiddling with his straw. 'I only say it to make Auntie Meryl mad. She's funny when she's mad. So who the bloody hell are you?' he added to Marika.

'Now that's enough, Rosencrantz!' I said. 'This is Marika, my new friend from school, and she is very nice.'

'Yes, you do look very nice, in fact you are very pretty,' said Rosencrantz, looking at Marika through his straw as if it were a telescope.

Marika smiled and blew down the straw.

'Got you,' she grinned.

'You did!' smiled Rosencrantz, offering her a crisp.

'You're in there, Marika,' said Daniel. 'He never offers anyone a crisp.'

I had started to relax and we were on our second round when Marika came with me to the cigarette machine. As I fed in two-pound coins and selected Marlboro Lights, I suddenly heard the *Thunderbirds* theme tune. We looked up at the TV in the corner of the bar. The Channel Four news headlines had just begun, and they were still running with the Tracy Island shortage.

'Bugger, bugger, bollocks!' I exclaimed, grabbing my fags out of the machine. 'I've left the bloody Tracy Island plans at school! I never got them from Mr Wednesday!'

'I thought you went to his classroom?'

'I did, long story.'

Marika checked her watch. 'Will anyone still be there?'

We looked at each other and realised not.

We went back over to the table and I gave Rosencrantz a pound, and told him to knock himself out on the Pac-Man machine in the corner. When he was out of earshot, I told Daniel what had happened, leaving out all the bits about Mr Wednesday not having his shirt on.

'Do you have the number for the caretaker?' asked Daniel.

'No, he's gone to Devon to see his sister,' said Marika. 'What about The Ripper?'

'Call him away from home on the first night he's had with his family in months? No way,' I said.

'I could phone him,' offered Marika.

'No, you don't want him getting funny with you. I think I could get in and out. I know a way into the school grounds and the back door to my classroom has a broken lock. It's usually open.'

'Break in?' said Daniel.

'It's not breaking in when the lock is broken already,' I pointed out

'You're mad, Coco,' he said.

'Am I?' I rounded on him. 'What I think I am is a desperate mother whose husband is laid up with a broken leg. We have nothing for Christmas, and I am not seeing our son's little face on Christmas Day anything other than happy.'

We looked over at Rosencrantz on the Pac-Man machine. He was standing on the small stool the landlord put there for the tiny kids, and his excited face was lit up by the yellow light of the game.

'Ok. What should I do?' he said.

'Just look after Rosencrantz.'

'I'll come with you,' said Marika, downing the rest of her wine.

'No, it's risky,' I told her.

'You are the first person in England who has treated me

like a friend and I always think you should help your friends, so let's go.'

Tony appeared in the doorway, looking in need of a drink.

'So this is where you're all hiding!' he grinned. 'Thought I'd leave Meryl to it, she's cleaning your skirting boards with a toothbrush.'

'Tony can help you hobble back across the road if we're gone for ages,' I said.

'Yes, will do!' said Tony.

I kissed Daniel on top of his head, slipped Tony a tenner for more drinks, and me and Marika went out into the darkness.

'How should we do this?' she asked as we picked our way along the pavement. It was now coated in a thin film of ice.

'We should go on foot,' I said. 'There's a gap in the side of the playing field fence.'

'How do you know?' asked Marika, moving faster to keep up with me.

'I overheard Kelly Roffey tell Damian Grange they could meet there.'

'Romantic...' said Marika.

When we arrived at St Dukes, the front gates were locked, and the orange street lights reflected off the bike sheds by the gate. The long squat building at the end of the drive was in darkness. We hurried past a row of terraced houses next to the school, and at the last house we turned down an alleyway leading along the perimeter of the school fields. It was dark and quiet.

'Coco!' hissed Marika. I turned and couldn't see her. 'Coco, I'm stuck,' she hissed again.

I tracked back to where Marika's coat was caught on a giant bramble, now dead but still with fearsome spikes.

'You should be able to pull free,' I whispered.

'This is my only coat,' she said.

I couldn't see her face properly but she sounded embarrassed. I gingerly grasped the long twisting bramble and unhooked Marika without doing her coat any damage. We carried on, down the side of the terraced houses, past dark gardens, and found the hole in the fence leading to the school playing fields. I held it open for Marika and she squeezed through. I followed and we ran, hunched over, across the wide, dark expanse of the school playing fields, towards the main school building.

We passed the long, tall windows of the assembly hall reflecting the wisps of cloud above, and then moved round to the art room. The huge chimney from the kiln cast its long shadow on the mini courtyard outside the door. I stopped and peered into the dark windows.

'Where could he have put it?' I said. Marika joined me at the window.

'Did he want to put it in your pigeon hole?' she asked.

'Yeah, but I told him I was married.'

'What?' she hissed.

'Oh. The pigeon holes by the main entrance, you mean. For internal mail. Yes, he might have.'

'Don't make me laugh, Coco, I'll wet myself,' she giggled.

I tried the door, but it was locked.

'We need to go round to my classroom,' I said.

We crouched down and ran along the back of the building, past the science labs and the school canteen where the bins were giving off a foul odour, even in the cold. We rounded the building and reached my classroom. I peered in the window. The room was dark and silent. I gripped the door handle and gently turned: the door opened a crack. Marika made to go in.

'You should stay outside,' I said. 'What if we get caught?'

'Who is going to catch you? The place is empty. There aren't burglar alarms, are there?'

'No,' I whispered. 'The Ripper never turns them on after they went off accidentally a few times one weekend.'

The door creaked as I opened it and we slipped inside. I closed it softly behind us, and we tiptoed between chairs stacked on rows of desks. Halfway along my handbag became tangled on a leg of one of the chairs and it fell off the table, hitting the floor with a crash. The door to my classroom was open and it echoed along the hall. We froze as the echo subsided. I was shaking and so was Marika.

'It's okay,' she whispered. 'We're the only ones here.'

Carefully I picked up the chair, turned it over and placed it gently back on the desk.

We crept out of my classroom and along the dark corridors. When we reached the doors to the assembly hall we stopped to catch our breath. I grimaced as the handle squealed, and the door creaked open. Long windows stretched all the way along one wall from floor to ceiling. The full moon lit the vast room.

'Let's be quick,' I whispered. 'It's so bright. People might see us!'

Halfway across the vast parquet floor of the hall, a huge cloud sailed in front of the moon, plunging us into darkness.

'I can't see anything!' whispered Marika.

I slowed and reached back, grabbing her hand. We fumbled our way to the other side of the hall, squealing when we made contact with the branches of the giant Christmas tree. We jumped back as it swayed and a lone bauble fell off, bouncing away on the dark floor like a ping-pong ball.

We finally made it out of the hall and along to Mr

Wednesday's classroom in the art department. The moon came back out and we approached Mr Wednesday's desk. There was nothing on it. The moonlight reflected off the polished wood. We stood for a moment looking at the driftwood of the abandoned still life.

'He probably put it in your pigeon hole then?' whispered Marika.

I gulped: the pigeonholes would mean another trip across the school to the front entrance. We slipped quietly out of the Art department, back through dark corridors. The school was starting to give me the creeps. All this empty space. Marika must have felt the same because she grabbed hold of my hand.

We arrived at the school canteen, passing rows of tables, and then we were through to the reception area. The wall of staff pigeonholes was opposite Miss Marks's desk. We were about to start poking around in the pigeonholes when we heard the main entrance door open and someone hit the lights. They blared on and we squinted against the brightness. Voices were coming towards us, fast, and we rushed down the corridor toward The Ripper's office. The door was closed but the little kitchenette opposite was open. We dived in and ducked down under a work surface to one side, between two big boxes of Styrofoam cups. We got there just in time as The Ripper walked past with Miss Marks!

Marika grabbed my hand again and dug her nails in. I bit my lip; we were both trembling. We heard the clinking of a big bunch of keys and The Ripper unlocked his office. They went inside, and the door closed. I leaned round the box, but the door opened again. I pressed my back against the wall. They stopped outside the kitchenette.

'How long have we got?' asked Miss Marks breathlessly. 'Will I get to see you over Christmas?'

Marika and I looked at each other outraged. Miss Marks was a home wrecker!

'You can come to my flat,' she went on. 'I put Mother down for a nap in the afternoons, so we'll have privacy.'

She sounded quite desperate.

'I want you. Now,' he growled.

'Where do you want to do it? The vaulting block in the gymnasium?' she suggested.

There was a slurping sound. Ugh. Miss Marks was kissing The Ripper!

'How about the biology lab? You want me to be your naughty gynaecologist?' growled The Ripper.

'*That's my classroom,*' mouthed Marika with a disgusted look on her face.

I was now terrified. What if they caught us? There were more slobbering, snogging noises and growling sounds. Then there was silence. We sat sweating for a few minutes, then a few minutes more. '*I'm going to look,*' I mouthed.

I peered round the boxes a fraction: they weren't in the doorway. I got up and slowly moved to the door, peeped round, but they had gone. I beckoned for Marika. We crept out and over to the pigeonholes. I found mine and, sure enough, tucked inside were the plans for Tracy Island.

'Let's get out of here,' said Marika, still terrified.

We made to leave, and then I noticed my Tracy Island on Miss Marks's desk! I went over to it and ran my finger along the cellophane. The box was so colourful, the picture of the toy island was so glossy and striking.

'This is what he must have come back for,' I said. 'He'd forgotten it.'

'Or he used it as an excuse to get out of the house,' said Marika.

'I went through so much to get this,' I said wistfully.

Making one out of old junk was going to be such a let-down for Rosencrantz. I looked over my shoulder and back at the box. I lifted it off the desk.

'You're going to take it?' gasped Marika.

'Why not? What can he prove?'

'Coco, you'd be crazy!'

'No, it's perfect, he hasn't seen us. He couldn't prove which member of staff it was.'

'But he knows you gave it to him and—'

'And what?' I interrupted.

I was going to do this. I was going to take it back from the cheating bastard. It was pleasingly heavy in my hand.

'They're coming back!' warned Marika.

Through the glass of the canteen doors The Ripper and Miss Marks came round the corner of the tables, walking hand in hand.

'Put it down Coco, and run!' hissed Marika.

Devastated, I put Tracy Island back and we ran, down the corridor and out of the front entrance, which thankfully was open. We dived through the hedges and ran across the playing fields to the gap in the fence, and then we were out and in the dark alley. We stopped to catch our breath. I was in tears.

'We got the plans, Coco,' said Marika, giving me a hug. But it didn't make me feel better.

We trudged past the terrace houses and towards the front of the school. Suddenly The Ripper's car was coming down the drive and approaching the school gates. We looked around for somewhere to hide. Then a hearse came purring out of the darkness and pulled up beside the kerb. The tinted window slid down.

'I thought you might need a getaway vehicle,' said Meryl,

leaning over to peer through the window, still wearing her curlers. 'Daniel and Tony came home and told me what you were up to.'

I yanked open the passenger door, but Marika hesitated. The Ripper's car was now almost at the gates.

'It's all right, dear, there's no dead body in the back. There was this morning, but she's now safely tucked away, six feet under,' trilled Meryl.

'Get in, Marika!' I hissed. We piled in and shut the door, just as The Ripper's car headlights reached us, illuminating the hearse.

'Where to?' asked Meryl, as if we'd just completed a bank heist.

'The pub,' I said, clutching the Tracy Island plans to my chest.

'Yes, I could do with a swift one. I am spitting feathers,' said Marika. We sank back against the leather seat in relief and laughed.

WEDNESDAY 23RD DECEMBER

It turned into quite a fun evening. We had some drinks and a bite to eat. Afterwards, I walked Marika over to Baker Street tube station and thanked her again for joining in the St Dukes heist.

'Think about coming for Christmas Day,' I said. 'I'd love you to be there.'

'No, Christmas is a time for family,' she said.

'Christmas is a time for wanting to kill my family,' I corrected her, but she wasn't having any of it. I watched as she went down the escalator and wished she wasn't so bloody proud.

When I got home, everyone was asleep. I kissed Rosencrantz good night and then found Daniel had returned to the marital bed, his plaster cast hanging off the end, and he was snoring loudly. I undressed, climbed in beside him and was asleep in seconds.

There was a knock on the bedroom door at six this morning. I thought it was Rosencrantz, but then I heard Meryl whispering, asking if I was 'decent'.

I left Daniel sleeping and came to the door. She was in her long button-up nightie and holding the plans for Tracy Island with her reading glasses perched on her nose.

'Coco, we need to talk,' she whispered.

'Now? It's early—'

'Now!,' insisted Meryl.

We came downstairs to the living room, and she closed the door, putting a chair under the door handle. On the sofa was a notebook full of her scribblings, and a video of *Blue Peter's* 'How to make Tracy Island' was paused on the television. All of Rosencrantz's Thunderbirds figures and toys were lined up on the coffee table.

'Where did you get that video from?'

'Mandy from Handy Mandy Crafts in Milton Keynes. Mandy was happy to help. She was very pleased with the job Tony did burying her mother.'

'That's very generous of her,' I said.

'Now, Coco. We're dealing with papier mâché,' said Meryl gravely.

'That's easy, isn't it? Just glue and old newspaper?' I said.

'Papier mâché may be slap-dash in its execution, but it needs time to dry. We've got barely forty-eight hours until Rosencrantz comes running down those stairs to see what Father Christmas has left him.'

I sat down heavily on the side of the sofa. I'd been so excited to get the plans last night that I'd forgotten we still had to make the damn thing.

'So we're screwed?' I said.

'Coco. No toilet language, please.'

'Sorry, Meryl.'

'I've watched the *Blue Peter* video and I've been planning,' said Meryl seriously. 'I think we can do it, but we can't waste any time. We need to make a couple of Tracy Islands, maybe three to cover ourselves.'

'Three?'

Meryl came and sat beside me.

'I've just been on the phone with Handy Mandy,' she said. 'Handy Mandy divulged to me her top-secret drying method for papier mâché.'

Meryl paused for dramatic effect.

'What is it?' I asked.

Meryl glanced around furtively, as if we were two ladies from the French Resistance hiding in a bunker.

'Bake it in the oven at eighty-five degrees for one hour,' she whispered. 'We'll need to monitor the temperature – any deviation from eighty-five degrees and the game's up. We can't take our eyes off it for a second. Are you with me Coco?'

I nodded seriously and tried to keep a straight face. She checked her watch.

'Right. You need to get dressed. We're going shopping.'

We were first at the supermarket when it opened at half past seven. As we dashed round with the trolley, I felt like an awful mother. Here I was with no present for Rosencrantz and attempting to make a substitute with ordinary household junk – washing-up liquid bottles, tin foil and old cardboard boxes, for God's sake! I had to thank Meryl for her steely resolve and for guiding the trolley round when the tears in my eyes blurred our route.

Meryl left me to go through the till, whilst she went to a pay phone and rang Ethel. We needed someone to keep Rosencrantz out of the house.

'Mum's not at home,' said Meryl when I wheeled the trolley out with all our purchases.

I was relieved. I didn't want to have to explain about Ethel boycotting the Nativity play.

'Chris is away on a cruise and Daniel's only got one good leg,' I said.

'It'll have to be Tony then,' shrugged Meryl.

'Tony?'

'Yes, it will do him good to spend some time with Rosencrantz, give him practice for...' Then Meryl was silent. She always dismissed the friendly enquiries she got about her having children, saying things like they'd just bought new carpets and a baby would cause havoc.

'So we'll get Tony babysitting,' she said, pulling herself together. 'Next stop B&Q.'

We arrived home just after ten, dragging bags full of Christmas shopping, Tracy Island shopping, and a six-foot Scotch pine in a bucket.

'Christmas tree! Yay!' yelled Rosencrantz.

He was disappointed when he heard he was going out for the day with Uncle Tony.

'Is he my uncle?' asked Rosencrantz.

'Of course he's your uncle!' said Meryl. 'He's married to me, and you know I'm your aunt.'

Rosencrantz looked surprised that the slightly pervy man who came every Christmas was related to him.

'What should I do with him?' I heard Tony whisper to Meryl.

'Get to know him, take him to the zoo or something,' hissed Meryl. 'Just bring him back in one piece.'

I nervously kissed Rosencrantz goodbye, and then Meryl

pulled me into the kitchen. She had laid everything out and was mixing up a gloopy paste in a bowl.

'Flour and water for the papier mâché,' she trilled. 'The *Blue Peter* Tracy Island starts with a square of cardboard from one of those big boxes from the supermarket. Then on top you build up layers and layers of papier mâché to make the shape of the island.'

It was slow, messy work, especially as we were making three islands. Daniel was helped down the stairs to reluctantly to lend a hand. Ever the practical one, Meryl made a lunch of cream cheese sandwiches with crisps, then washed the tubs up for the next phase of Tracy Island. The control tower lookout was made from an upside down cream cheese tub with square stickers to form windows.

By mid-afternoon the kitchen was a mess of flour and water paste and scrunched-up newspaper, but we had finished the main work on three Tracy Islands. One went into the oven on a very low heat, whilst the other two went upstairs into the airing cupboard.

We'd just finished clearing away the glue and paste when Tony came through the front door with Rosencrantz. Tony was soaking wet, and his lips were blue.

'My godfathers! What happened?' cried Meryl, pulling him into the living room.

'He fell in the Emperor penguin pond,' said Rosencrantz matter-of-factly.

'Emperor Penguin pond?' asked Meryl

'L-L-London Z-Z-Zoo,' shivered Tony.

'He got pecked a lot too!' said Rosencrantz gleefully.

I noticed peck marks on Tony's nose, and on top where his hair was thinning. I grabbed him a blanket off the sofa, and

Daniel hobbled over to the fire and attempted to put some more wood on.

'Daniel, sit down,' I snapped. 'We can't have any more accidents!'

'Tony! Come upstairs and get those wet clothes off,' instructed Meryl.

Tony shuddered as she led him out of the room and up the stairs.

'Did you know Uncle Tony buries dead people in the ground?' said Rosencrantz. 'And if they don't want to pay extra for him to dig a hole, he burns them in a big oven!'

'Well, it's a bit nicer than that,' said Daniel.

'The oven!' I cried, noticing a faint burning smell.

Rosencrantz sniffed the air.

'Oh Mummy, are you cooking again?' he said, sounding dismayed.

'What do you mean?'

'Well, it *always* goes wrong!'

'Oh no! The Tr—' I stopped myself in time and ran into the kitchen, just as the fire alarm began to beep. The room was filled with smoke and a hideous burning smell. I yanked open the oven, and black smoke poured out, spreading across the ceiling. Without thinking I grabbed the grill pan and pain shot through my hand. I dropped it on the floor and ran to the sink, plunging my hand under the cold water.

'What was *that*, Mummy? I'm not eating it!' said Rosencrantz, peering at the remains of the Tracy Island that never was, the top blackened and the bottom a saggy, glutinous mess.

'Ow, ow, ow! Shepherd's pie,' I lied.

Rosencrantz gave me a look. Then we heard a scream from

upstairs, and feet thundering down the stairs. Meryl rushed in, her head covered in what looked like grey vomit.

'Quick, move. I need water! Before it sets!' cried Meryl, running over to the sink. She shoved her head under the tap and turned on the water. 'I went to the airing cupboard to get towels for Tony,' she hissed at me, pulling what I now realised were gloopy lumps of papier mâché out of her hair. 'I forgot what we'd put in there to dry, and they both came tumbling out and landed on my head!'

'Both of them!'

'Yes! They're both ruined. Oh, it's setting!' she cried. 'If this flour and water paste sets in my hair, I'll never get it out! I'll have to shave my head!'

'I can't believe Uncle Tony buries people in the ground, and gets paid for it!' said Rosencrantz, oblivious to the chaos. 'I was going to ask him if he'd ever buried anyone alive by mistake but he fell in the penguin pond...'

We put Tony, Rosencrantz and Daniel in the living room and got to work on clearing up the mess. It took two hours. The carpet on the landing would have to be replaced, and poor Meryl didn't get to the sink fast enough. Her hair set into a solid, spivvy quiff. At four-thirty we sat with a stiff whiskey and a cigarette each, even though Meryl doesn't usually smoke, and we made a plan.

1. Buy new materials and start again from scratch.
2. Leave the menfolk here with money/telephone numbers to order a take away.
3. Move Tracy Island operations to Chris's house. He has a huge double catering oven he never uses, a sauna, and one of those upright salon hairdryers

you can sit under. All of which could come in
useful drying papier mâché.

Rosencrantz was quite excited when I said that Daniel and
Tony would be looking after him.

'I'm going to ask Uncle Tony loads of questions,' he
grinned. 'Do you think he'd take me on a trip to Milton Keynes
to see some dead bodies?'

'Well, maybe that's not the nicest thing to do at Christmas,'
I said.

'Yes,' he agreed sagely. 'What about the day after Boxing
Day?'

I kissed him and promised we'd have lots of time
tomorrow.

I packed an overnight bag, lent Meryl a baseball cap and
we set off for Chris's house, unsure of when we would return.

THURSDAY 24TH DECEMBER
(CHRISTMAS EVE)

Meryl was quite enchanted by all the Disneyana at Chris's house. We spent most of the night working in his huge kitchen, making three new Tracy Islands. The first perished in the oven, but the amazing news was that the second and third fared much better in Chris's walk-in sauna. The dry, hot atmosphere was perfect, and as of three o'clock in the afternoon the papier mâché was drying nicely.

I was making us a well-deserved cup of coffee in the kitchen, when I heard Meryl talking in the hall. Then she poked her quiffed head round the door with the phone held against her cardigan,

'Coco! What's this about you banning Mum from Rosencrantz's school Nativity play?'

She put the phone back to her ear,

'What's that? No, I know, Mum. You'd never smoke in Rosencrantz's bedroom... Of course I'm fine. You didn't know about the effects when you were expecting us.'

Meryl listened then put the phone back to her cardigan.

'Coco! The top of my head wasn't flat when I was a baby!' I looked at Meryl with her rock-hard quiff of hair.

'Well, I might have been a little angry,' I said 'but I never banned her from—'

Meryl put the phone back to her ear.

'What, Mum? You're not coming to Coco's for Christmas... You're going to stop at home and eat Spam salad!' She handed me the phone. 'She wants to talk to you.'

I took the phone. 'Ethel?' I said.

'I ain't settin' foot over yer threshold. I know when I'm not wanted,' she said, and she hung up!

We tried to ring her back, but we kept getting the engaged tone.

'I think you need to sort this out, Coco,' said Meryl sternly.

'Look, me and your mother don't see eye to eye, that's not a secret,' I said.

'Coco, Mum thinks the world of you! I wonder if it's you with the problem?'

I went to protest but Meryl raised a hand.

'Why don't you drive over to Catford? Explain truthfully how much you want Mum to be there on Christmas Day.'

'Truthfully?'

'Yes, Coco. It wouldn't be Christmas without her. Now go. I'm the craft expert. I'll stay here and supervise Tracy Island.'

It was gone six o'clock when I pulled up at Ethel's house in Catford. The street lights were broken so the row of grimy terraced houses was doused in gloom. A distant police siren screamed, and the windows leading away from Ethel's house were all dark. There was a tiny glow coming from behind the curtains in her front room.

I took the passage along the side of the house. The light

was on in the kitchen, casting a rectangle of yellow in the back yard. I went up to the door and banged on the glass.

'Oo is it?' came her voice a moment later.

'It's Coco,' I said.

There was a pause.

'I've got nothing to say to yer!' she shouted.

'That's a first,' I said. 'Seems you've had plenty to say over the years.'

I hammered again on the door.

'I'm not going until you open up, we need to have this out!' I shouted.

A minute later Ethel opened the door. She was wearing her flowery housecoat and had a fag on the go. She dragged me inside.

'Jeez, keep yer voice down! The neighbours'll think I've got the bailiff round, or, worse, that I'm behind on me catalogue payments!'

'I do not look like a bailiff,' I said.

'They come in all shapes and sizes: small and, in your case, big.'

The kitchen, as ever, was warm and cosy. A little fire was glowing in the hearth and Christmas cards were dotted along the mantelpiece. A clock in the middle chimed the quarter hour, and I could see her rent book poking out from behind.

'That's enough. I've had enough of you, Ethel. I've tried and I've tried until I'm blue in the face. You don't like me – I get it. And you know what? I don't much like you. All I've ever done is love your son. All I've ever got is nastiness from you. And as for not coming to the Nativity play... Well, it ends now, you hear me?'

Ethel regarded me for a moment and took a drag on her cigarette.

'You want a cup of tea, love?' she asked.

'Didn't you hear what I said?'

'Or something stronger?'

'I'm driving,' I said, exasperated.

She ignored me and left the room, coming back with two large schooners and a bottle of sherry. She poured two glasses.

'Sit down, love,' she said. I pulled out a chair at the blue Formica table. 'Not the ripped one,' she added. I pulled out the chair beside it and sat. We both took a sip.

'I will say I'm sorry. I know you weren't smoking in Rosencrantz's room.'

'An' I never would,' she said. We drank in silence.

'Look, why don't we just agree that we don't like each other and then move on.'

'I don't dislike yer, love.'

'Then what?'

'I just don't wanna lose me son.'

'You haven't lost your son, believe me.'

We took another sip. I went on.

'I wish you'd come to Rosencrantz's Nativity play. It's not on that you used it to make a point. You can throw as much shit as you like at me, but don't you dare upset Rosencrantz.'

For the first time ever, I saw Ethel looked chastised.

'Sorry, love. So 'ow was it?'

I told her about Rosencrantz's Nativity play. Ethel burst out laughing. It emerged with a rattle from her chest. She threw her head back and slapped her leg.

'I'd 'ave given anything to 'ear your little Rosencrantz say *I'm not a pleasant fucker* during a Nativity play! Must've brightened it up for all the parents.'

'Yes, well...'

'Did Chris tape it?'

'No, he didn't video the performance.'

'Performance! I'll say,' she squawked, dissolving into even more laughter, which then turned into a coughing fit.

I couldn't help it, I began to laugh too.

'Oh Coco. What am I gonna do with you?' she said when we'd calmed down a bit.

'What do you mean?'

'You're a resilient cow.'

'Thanks.'

'You remember when you first came in this kitchen?'

'Yes.'

'All those years ago. I thought you was wet, a right wet weekend. But you've proved yerself you can be a tough old mare.'

'How is *any* of that a compliment?' I asked.

'You need to be tough in this life. I know my Danny can be pretty useless,' she said, 'but 'is heart is in the right place. 'E just needs nurturing, 'e'll come good.'

'I've nurtured him for years, and I'm still the breadwinner,' I said. 'I thought when we had Rosencrantz things would change.'

'The slowest tree bears the best fruit, Coco.'

'But I'm worried we'll starve before he produces anything edible,' I said.

Ethel poured us more sherry.

'Maybe it's my fault. Maybe that ashtray squashed all the good brain cells,' she said with a grin.

'Look, Ethel. It would make Rosencrantz and Daniel, and Meryl and Tony... and *me* very happy if you'd come for Christmas tomorrow.'

'Tomorrow? I'm coming tonight! I ain't gonna get on a bus tomorrow.'

'What?'

'I always stay up your place on Christmas Eve, Coco. It's tradition!'

'So you were coming all along?' I said.

'Course I was love, and now you're here, you can give me a lift.'

Before I could say any more, Ethel bolted upstairs and returned with her suitcase and a Tesco bag full of wrapped presents. I'd been lured over as a bloody taxi!

As we crossed the river, the fairy lights on Chelsea Bridge shifted and clattered in the breeze. I drove slowly along the embankment so we could look at all the houses with Christmas trees in the window. I realised my house was far from looking Christmassy.

As we approached Piccadilly Circus, it began to snow. At first it was blown across the road like icing sugar, but it quickly began to settle. As we turned the corner by the huge statue of Eros, last-minute shoppers were lugging bags, rugged up against the swirling snow. The Christmas lights were beautiful, and their reflections moved slowly across the windscreen.

The traffic lights turned red, and a swarm of shoppers spilled off the kerb weaving through the stationary traffic. The huge signs advertising Coca Cola and TDK changed the eddying snow from red to blue and back again.

''Ere, Coco love, iss gonna be a white Christmas after all,' said Ethel looking up in wonderment.

When we got home the house had been transformed. It was warm and clean. A fire was burning, and there was a Christmas tree glittering with lights and decorations.

'We made ourselves useful,' said Tony, red in the face from whiskey. The peck marks on his head were now turning purple. He hitched up his trousers and gave me a kiss on the cheek.

'And I made Daddy a crotch!' said Rosencrantz, indicating Daniel standing by the tree with the broom under his arm.

'It's a crutch, love,' said Daniel. I went over to him and he hugged me. 'Thanks for going and getting, Mum,' he added.

'Coco kindly invited me for Christmas, an' I accepted,' said Ethel, surprising me with a smile.

Daniel handed me a bauble.

'Thought we'd leave this one for you,' he said. He held up the glass bauble with *Karen* written on it.

'You remembered,' I grinned. I found a branch and hung it on.

'There. Now it's Christmas,' said Daniel, and leant across and gave me a kiss.

We stood admiring the twinkling lights and decorations for a moment, then Rosencrantz asked, 'Who's Karen?'

'It's Mummy's real name,' said Daniel. 'Coco is a nickname I gave her.'

'Then who gave Mummy her real name?'

'Her mummy and daddy...' explained Daniel.

'No. Dad wanted to call me Jessica, but Mum overruled him on that, as she did with most things,' I said.

'They're dead, aren't they?' asked Rosencrantz.

'Yes. They are,' I said. There was silence.

'So did you have them burned in Uncle Tony's special

oven for dead bodies, or did you pay extra and dig a hole to put them in?' asked Rosencrantz in a chatty little tone of voice.

'Rosencrantz!' snapped Daniel.

'Rosencrantz... *Rosencrantz*,' said Rosencrantz, as if he'd heard his name for the first time. 'Have I got a proper real name too? Cos Rosencrantz, it's a bit bloody weird!'

'No toilet language!' trilled Meryl, bustling into the living room wearing a Santa hat. She hugged me and Ethel. 'It's no use,' she said. 'I'll have to have my hair cut off, it's still rock-hard after four *Wash and Go's*.'

'She washed it and it went nowhere!' piped up Rosencrantz.

Just then the downstairs toilet flushed. I looked around the room.

'Who else is here?' I said.

Marika came sheepishly into the living room.

'I only phoned to talk to you, Coco,' she said, embarrassed.

'Her teeth were chatting away!' said Rosencrantz excitedly, and he did an impression of a very cold person shivering. 'I told her she had to come for Christmas. She can sleep in my bed,' he added.

'I invited Marika to come over, too,' said Daniel. Marika still looked embarrassed.

'I'm so glad you're here!' I said giving her a hug.

'She brought some rather delicious Slovak cakes,' added Tony.

'Yeah Mummy, they're like Jammy Dodgers!' said Rosencrantz.

'And I will help out with cooking, cleaning—' offered Marika.

'No you won't, you're my guest and my friend, and I'm so pleased you're here,' I said.

Meryl beckoned me and Marika out of the living room. Ethel came too, and we followed her upstairs. She checked the coast was clear and opened the airing cupboard door. On the bottom shelf was a complete Tracy Island! It looked stunning, almost like the real thing.

'The paint just needs the night to harden,' said Meryl.

'It's beautiful,' I said, marvelling at the detail – the palm trees made from pipe cleaners, the green hills of the island and the beach, and the swimming pool, made from a circle of tin foil.

'Thank you, Meryl,' I said, hugging her, almost in tears.

'Yes well, I wanted to tick it off my list, craft wise,' she said embarrassed.

'Tha's lovely, Meryl,' said Ethel. 'Oh Coco, 'e's gonna love that.'

'It's beautiful,' added Marika.

'This is amazing, Meryl,' I said. 'But do you think Rosencrantz will mind it's not the shop version?'

'Don't be silly, love' said Ethel. 'Iss like that Dolly Parton song.'

We looked at her, confused.

'You know, that Dolly Parton song, where she sings about that jumper 'er Mum made 'er... with all them bits of wool lying around. In all different colours... cos they 'ad no money.'

"The Coat of Many Colours",' said Marika.

'Oh, was it a coat love? What was the song called?' said Ethel.

"The Coat of Many Colours",' I repeated.

'No, Marika's established that, Coco, love, but what was the song called?'

"The Coat of Many Colours",' we all chimed, but Ethel ignored us.

'No, it's got a really good name. I've got it! 'Jolene's Amazing Technicolour Dreamcoat'!'

We all managed to stifle a laugh. Ethel went on,

'Dolly Parton sings 'ow much she loves Jolene's amazing technicolour dream coat. An' she loves it, cos 'er Mum made it for 'er. It was all the more special, you know? An' it'll be the same thing with Rosencrantz. Cos you all made it for 'im.'

'Thanks Ethel,' I said.

'To think Dolly Parton's mum's name was Jolene,' she added. 'Cos then she wrote that song about Jolene nicking 'er usband off 'er! They're a funny lot in America, aren't they?'

We all grinned.

The last few hours of Christmas Eve were wonderful. We lit a fire, ordered pizza and Daniel played carols on the piano, with his leg propped up on the portable electric heater.

It was so lovely to have Marika here too. She fitted in with everyone and she was a big hit with Rosencrantz. He spent the whole evening brushing her hair and asking her to teach him Slovakian swear words.

I came to bed relieved. We'd done it. Rosencrantz was going to open Tracy Island on Christmas Day, just as he wanted.

FRIDAY 25TH DECEMBER (CHRISTMAS DAY)

I slept soundly until the alarm beeped softly at a quarter to six. I turned to wish Daniel a merry Christmas but his side of the bed was empty. It was chilly, so I pulled on a jumper and tiptoed out to the landing. I could hear noises from the bathroom, and assumed that must be where Daniel was. I opened the airing cupboard and took a moment to admire the beautiful Tracy Island once more. I tried the paint with the tips of my fingers, and it was bone dry. I decided it was time to wrap it. Checking Rosencrantz's door was shut I very gently lifted it out of the airing cupboard, then turned carefully holding it in both hands. I heard the bathroom door open and the sound of Daniel clunking across the carpet.

Seconds later the airing cupboard door was shoved closed against my back. I was knocked into the shelves inside and Tracy Island crumpled as it was crushed between the shelves and the front of my jumper. I squealed in shock. Daniel pulled the airing cupboard door open and the crushed pieces of Tracy Island fell to the carpet. A big chunk was caught in the fibres of my jumper. We both froze.

'You idiot!' I hissed.

'Oh no! Coco! I, I... The door was open!' said Daniel.

'So you closed it without checking?'

'I didn't think,' he said.

'You never bloody do. Your mother was right about that ashtray!'

'Ashtray?' echoed Daniel.

I looked down at the wreckage of Tracy Island and burst into tears. Ethel came out onto the landing rubbing her eyes. Her face fell.

'Your son shut the door on me!'

'What did you do that for, yer bloody idiot!' said Ethel, giving him a slap round the head.

'I've got a broken leg!'

'I'm tempted to break the other one, you prat!' said Ethel.

Then Meryl came out of the spare room.

'What's going on? It's six o'clock on Christmas morning, I don't want to hear toilet language!' She saw the Tracy Island wreckage. 'You bloody idiot, Daniel!' she shrieked.

Tony and then Marika joined us. We were paralysed, not knowing what to do.

Then Rosencrantz's door opened. I quickly closed the airing cupboard door after pushing all the bits on the carpet inside too.

'Happy Christmas everyone!' said Rosencrantz, grinning. 'Can I open my presents?'

There was an awkward pause.

'Let's see if we can spot Father Christmas flying across the sky!' said Ethel, grabbing him and taking him back in his bedroom.

'I thought he comes during the night?' said Rosencrantz.

'Oh 'e does, but 'e knocks off at six and 'as a quick pint

before 'e goes off to Lapland. Maybe 'e's bin at the pub at the end of the road.' She managed to get him in his room and shut the door.

'Coco, have we got anything else we can give Rosencrantz instead?' begged Daniel.

'That is the most stupid question I've ever heard!' I said, seething with rage. I ignored him, came downstairs and into the living room. The presents were all laid out under the tree.

'Ooh look, is that Father Christmas's reindeer in the beer garden?' I heard Ethel say from upstairs in Rosencrantz's bedroom.

Marika joined me in the living room and saw my tears.

'Oh God, Marika. What are we going to do?'

She gave me a hug. Then Rosencrantz bolted downstairs, past us and into the living room shouting, 'Presents, present, presents!'

Ethel appeared out of breath at the door.

'I couldn't keep 'old of 'im. 'E's like a slippery little bar of soap.'

Within seconds, Rosencrantz had the wrapping paper off four of his presents. He was wild with excitement.

'Slow down, love,' I pleaded.

I felt powerless, a failure. I came out of the living room and shut the door. Ethel, Marika, Meryl and Tony were in the hall. Daniel was hobbling downstairs.

'I can't watch him get to the last present,' I said. 'I'm going to be sick.'

Just then the doorbell rang. We all froze for a moment. It rang again.

'Well, someone answer it,' said Ethel. 'It ain't bloody Father Christmas!'

I pulled open the door. There stood Chris, crying. In his hand he held... a Tracy Island!

'What? How?' I said with wonder.

'I know I should be on the cruise, but I jumped ship. Well, not literally, I can't swim. I waited until we docked at Calais and got a ferry back. I've broken up with Benji,' sobbed Chris.

We all stared at him in shock.

'I know, I can see what you're all thinking. I said I thought he was the one, but the 'cruise' he'd booked us on was a bloody Disney Christmas Cruise! I said I am NOT going to be trapped on a boat with a bunch of Disney freaks!'

'Um, is that Tracy Island?' I asked, insensitively I know.

'What?' said Chris.

'Tracy Island?' said Meryl.

'Tracy bleedin' Island?' said Ethel.

Chris looked confused.

'IS THAT TRACY ISLAND?' we all shouted.

'Oh, this? Yes,' said Chris, holding up the box. 'Dad got one in the end, from his friend in the import-export biz. Had it delivered to my house last night.'

Meryl lunged at the box and grabbed it out of Chris's hand.

'Give me two minutes! Tony!' she barked, clicking her fingers. 'I need a yard of red ribbon, Sellotape, scissors, and that roll of nice wrapping paper.'

They vanished upstairs. Chris looked bewildered.

'It's just a toy,' he said.

'Chris, if you expect to live long enough to see the Queen's Speech you will take that back. It is not just a toy. It's an embodiment of everything: my ability to be a good mother and to make my son happy.'

'Cokes, you're scaring me,' he said.

'Sorry. It's so good to see you!' I dragged him in off the step and hugged him.

Meryl was back down the stairs in two minutes with Tracy Island wrapped. We all crept into the living room to find Rosencrantz sitting amongst a pile of discarded wrapping paper.

'Where did Father Christmas put my big present?' he asked.

'Look behind the tree, love,' said Ethel.

'I did look, Nan,' answered Rosencrantz.

'Well, look again, 'ere, I'll help.'

She took him up to the Christmas tree, and when their backs were turned I gently placed the wrapped Tracy Island on top of the unwrapped presents. Rosencrantz turned and his eyes lit up when he saw the box with the big bow.

'Wow! You just missed him,' I said.

'He just whipped in the door and whipped out again, like lightning,' said Daniel.

'Really?' said Rosencrantz.

'Yes, Father Christmas moves very fast,' nodded Meryl.

'How do you think he gets round all the houses?' said Tony.

'See love, I told you'd 'e'd bin in the pub,' smiled Ethel.

The look of wonder on Rosencrantz's face made everything melt away – all the stress and the panic, all the anger and fear. He seized the present and tore off the paper.

'Tracy Island!' he cried. 'This is the best bloody Christmas ever!'

Tears began to roll down my face and I looked round at Marika and Chris smiling, at Daniel with his leg in plaster, Meryl with her hair frozen in a rock-hard Elvis quiff, Tony covered in peck marks from his brush with the Emperor penguins, Ethel grinning without her teeth, and me with the tail end of a black eye and bits of green papier mâché all down me. Outside there was a deep blanket of snow, and I was inside, safe and warm with the people I loved.

'Yes, it's the best Christmas ever,' I said.

And I meant it.

A NOTE FROM ROBERT

Hello, and a huge thank you for choosing to read *Coco Pinchard's Must-Have Toy Story*. If you did enjoy it, I would be very grateful if you could tell your friends and family. Word-of-mouth is one of the most effective ways of recommending a book, and it helps me reach out and find new readers. Your endorsement makes a big difference! You could also write a product review. It needn't be long, just a few words, but this also helps new readers find one of my books for the first time.

If you want to get in touch, you can find me via my website, www.robertbryndza.com.

And to all the parents, guardians, and anyone who is in pursuit of the must-have toy this Christmas. Stay safe, and don't do anything too crazy trying to get it. And just remember, however great the toy is, they will probably end up playing with the box!

Robert Bryndza

ABOUT THE AUTHOR

Robert Bryndza is an international bestselling author, best known for his page-turning crime and thriller novels, which have sold over four million copies in the English language.

His crime debut, *The Girl in the Ice* was released in February 2016, introducing Detective Chief Inspector Erika Foster. Within five months it sold one million copies, reaching number one in the Amazon UK, USA and Australian charts. To date, *The Girl in the Ice* has sold over 1.5 million copies in the English language and has been sold into translation in 29 countries. It was nominated for the Goodreads Choice Award for Mystery & Thriller (2016), the Grand prix des lectrices de Elle in France (2018), and it won two reader voted awards, The Thrillzone Awards best debut thriller in The Netherlands (2018) and The Dead Good Papercut Award for best page turner at the Harrogate Crime Festival (2016).

Robert has released a further five novels in the Erika Foster series, *The Night Stalker, Dark Water, Last Breath, Cold Blood* and *Deadly Secrets*, all of which have been global bestsellers, and in 2017 *Last Breath* was a Goodreads Choice Award nominee for Mystery and Thriller.

Most recently, Robert created a new crime thriller series based around the central character Kate Marshall, a police officer turned private detective. The first book, *Nine Elms*, was an Amazon USA #1 bestseller and an Amazon UK top five bestseller, and the series has been sold into translation in 15 countries. The second book, *Shadow Sands* was an Amazon charts and Wall Street Journal bestseller, and the third book, *Darkness Falls* will be published shortly.

Robert was born in Lowestoft, on the east coast of England. He studied at Aberystwyth University, and the Guildford School of Acting, and was an actor for several years, but didn't find success until he took a play he'd written to the Edinburgh Festival. This led to the decision to change career and start writing. He self-published a bestselling series of romantic comedy novels, before switching to writing crime. Robert lives with his husband in Slovakia, and is lucky enough to write full-time.

Printed in Great Britain
by Amazon

25866335R10081